THE LAST DAY OF A CONDEMNED MAN

and

CLAUDE GUEUX

BY VICTOR HUGO

"L'idée a qui tout céde et qui toujours éclaire
Prouve sa sainteté même dans sa colére.
Elle laisse toujours les principes debout.
Être vainqueurs, c'est peu, mais rester grands, c'est tout.
Quand nous tiendrons le traitre, abject, frissonnant, blème,
Affirmons le progrès dans le châtiment même."

Victor Hugo.

A Digireads.com Book
Digireads.com Publishing

The Last Day of a Condemned Man and Claude Gueux
By Victor Hugo
Translated by C. E. Wilbour
ISBN 10: 1-4209-3895-9
ISBN 13: 978-1-4209-3895-1

This edition copyright © 2010

Please visit *www.digireads.com*

CONTENTS

THE TRANSLATOR TO THE READER.

p. 5

CLAUDE GUEUX.

p. 11

THE LAST DAY OF A CONDEMNED MAN.

p. 29

4

THE TRANSLATOR TO THE READER.

To undertake a task so difficult, and perhaps beyond my ability, that of translating one of M. Victor Hugo's works, is to recognize the necessity of entering into an explanation with the reader, and of endeavoring to obtain his confidence. The fact of having selected "Claude Gueux" from so many works (where to choose would seem so difficult) indicates premeditation and a particular object in view. What is "Claude Gueux?" "Claude Gueux" is an ardent, vehement, and impassioned narrative, overflowing with an immense love for humanity, a vigorous hatred for social crimes, and a lofty indignation for official hypocrisies. "Claude Gueux" is the ghastly and blood-stained truth, hurled, in all its horror, at the head of a civilization that must one day, sooner or later, depart and give place to a more softened and to a higher civilization; "Claude Gueux" is one of the numerous pleadings of Victor Hugo against the scaffold, and for the inviolability of human life. And, as it is true that the hideous philosophy which stains the pages of penal codes immerses humanity in darkness, equally true is it that the philosophy full of enlightenment, peace, gentleness, and love, which distinguishes these eloquent pages, is as the dawn succeeding the darkness. It is because "Claude Gueux" is a striking, a terrible, a victorious argument against capital punishment, that I have translated it, at a time when almost all intelligent minds are occupied with this great question, upon which the attention of some of the most profound thinkers has long been fixed.

While I am writing, the question of the abolition of capital punishment is under consideration in England. The House of Commons and the Government have been set in motion by public opinion. It behoves, therefore, every heart that beats in unison for this great principle, every mind that has hitherto worked for and hoped for its ultimate triumph, now to come forward and take part in the final struggle.

If, in one of the scales of the balance, for so many ages of barbarism, there has rested the false weight that has been called "Justice," it is now time to place in the other scale the just weight, which is justice tempered with mercy and combined with moral improvement.

A Royal Commission has been appointed, and is now sitting. Important results have thus been obtained. Already inquiries, sincerely followed up, begin to throw light upon the subject. This is why I have desired to bring my stone (however small and poor a one it may be) to assist in the building of the great edifice, the foundations of which are already laid, in offering to the English public the work, so full of light, of this winning and noble genius.

Yes, there is light there! It shines with the powerful radiance of goodness and truth. Let those who read and feel it, *act*.

There is no question of taking the gallows by storm. No. The gallows must be judged with calmness by the conscience of the whole nation. It must be condemned, in its turn. "We must one day see it in some museum, the relic of a bygone and barbarous age, with the inscription, "Broken up and cut to pieces' for its crimes."

M. "Victor Hugo publishes, at the head of "Claude Gueux," a simple and unaffected letter, which I think is appropriate, and which perhaps inspired me with the idea now reduced to a fact,—that is to say, the present translation.

This letter is preceded by the following reflection,—

"The letter given below, the original of which is deposited at the office of the 'Revue de Paris,' does its author too much honor not to be reproduced by us here. It is united henceforth to all reimpressions of Claude Gueux." [1]

[1] "La lettre ci-dessous, dont l'original est déposé aux bureaux de la *Revue de Paris*, fait trop d'honneur à son auteur pour que nous ne la reproduisions pas ici. Elle est désormais liée à toutes les réimpressions de *Claude Gueux*."

It is thus seen that our duty has been marked out for us prospectively by the illustrious author "himself. This is the letter,—
"Dunkerque, *the 30th of July*, 1834.
"*To the Director of the 'Revue de Paris,*'
"'Claude Gueux,' by Victor Hugo, inserted by you in your number of the 6th instant, is a great lesson; aid me, I pray you, in making it profitable.
"Render me the service, I beg of you, of causing to be printed at my expense, as many copies as there are deputies in France, and of forwarding them to them individually and very exactly.
"With compliments,
"Charles Carlier, Négociant." [2]

[2] "Dunkerque, le 30 *juillet*, 1834.
"*M. le Directeur de la 'Revue de Paris'*
"'*Claude Gueux*,' de Victor Hugo, par vous inséré dans votre livraison du 6 courant, est une grande leçon; aidez-moi, je vous prie, à la faire profiter.
"Rendez-moi, je vous prie, le service d'en faire tirer, à mes frais, autant d'exemplaires qu'il y a de députés en France, et de les leur adresser individuellement et bien exactement.
"J'ai l'honneur de vous saluer,
"Charles Carlier, Négociant."

It will be understood by these few lines what a great effect the publication of "Claude Gueux" produced at the time, and it will be the more readily understood from the fact that this story is not a work of imagination, but a true narrative, every incident in which occurred exactly as the author tells it; all that is added is the magic of his style and the expression of his profound and tender sympathy for those classes which seem to be disinherited, one may almost say, in the present ill-adjusted state of society.

But it required all the fervor of my conviction and all the enthusiasm which for a long time I have felt for this question, which is one of the first of questions, to embolden me to undertake the translation of one of M. Victor Hugo's works. An *absolute* translation of this immense writer is impossible, and most applicable to him is the saying so often repeated by Byron in his indignation against French and other translators, *traduttore, traditore*. With the exception, perhaps, of the translation of the last work of the illustrious poet, a work dedicated to England, "William Shakespeare," a grave reproach is to be made against the English translators of this great writer; they have translated for the sake of translating, without sufficient regard for that magnificent language, which is a language of his own, and which his school only as yet begin to lisp. They have dared, as I do today, to venture into the midst of these vigorous sentences, each word of which is an image, a splendid and necessary accompaniment to a thought always profound.

Yes, it is after having translated Victor Hugo, that I declare him to be untranslatable; and I cannot better explain my meaning than by quoting here what Victor Hugo himself says of the translation of Shakespeare, in the brilliant preface which has just been published to the admirable translation of the works of *Shakespeare* by his son M. François Victor Hugo (*Œuvres complètes de W. Shakespeare*); this translation he declares to be the one that belongs to the future, because it is the only one which respects and is faithful to the text of our great poet.

First, there is an estimation of translations in general, [3]—

[3] "Une traduction est presque toujours regardée tout d'abord pax le peuple à qui on la donne, comme une violence qu'on lui fait.

Une langue dans laquelle on transvase de la sorte un autre idiome, fait ce qu'elle peut pour refuser.

Cette saveur nouvelle lui répugne. Ces locutions insolites, ces tours inattendus, cette irruption sauvage de figures inconnues—tout cela, c'est de l'invasion.

C'est de la poésie en excès. Il y a là abus d'images, profusion de métaphores, violation des frontières, introduction forcée du goût cosmopolite dans le gout local."

"A translation is almost always regarded, at first sight, by the people to whom it is given, as a violence done to them.

A language into which one decants, in a manner, another idiom does what it can to resist.

This novel savor is repugnant to it. These unusual expressions, these unexpected turns, this fierce inroad of unknown figures,—all that is invasion.

It is poetry in excess. There is there abuse of images, profusion of metaphors, violation of frontiers, the forced introduction of cosmopolitan taste into the local taste."

After these reflections on translations in general, M. Victor Hugo passes directly to Shakespeare, and it must be said "here, that everything that he advances regarding Shakespeare is applicable to himself. [4] "To translate Shakespeare," he says,—

[4] "Traduire Shakespeare, le traduire réellement, le traduire avec confiance, le traduire en s'abandonnant à lui, le traduire avec la simplicité honnôte et fière de l'enthousiasme, ne rien éluder, ne rien omettre, ne rien amortir, ne rien cacher, ne pas lui mettre de voile là où il est nu, ne pas lui mettre de masque là où il est sincère, ne pas lui prendre sa peau pour mentir dessous, le traduire sans recourir à la périphrase, cette restriction mentale, le traduire sans complaisance puriste pour la France ou puritaine pour l'Angleterre, dire la vérité, toute la vérité, rien que la vérité, le traduire comme on témoigne, ne point le trahir, l'introduire à Paris de plain pied, ne pas prendre de précautions insolentes pour ce génie, proposer à la moyenne des intelligences, qui a la prétention de s'appeler le goût, l'acceptation de ce géant: Le voila! en voulez-vous? ne pas crier gare, ne pas être honteux du grand homme, l'avouer, l'afficher, le proclamer, le promulguer, être sa chair et ses os, prendre son empreinte, mouler sa forme, penser sa pensée, parler sa parole, répercuter Shakespeare de l'anglais en français—quelle entreprise!

"Shakespeare est un des poëtes qui se défendent le plus contre le traducteur.

Il échappe par l'idée, il échappe par l'expression.

Quelle intrépidité il faut pour reproduire nettement en français certaines beautés insolentes de ce poëte, par exemple, le *buttock of the night*, où l'on entrevoit les parties honteuses de l'ombre. D'autres expressions semblent sans équivalents possibles; ainsi *green girl, fille verte*, n'a aucun sens en français. On pourrait dire de certains mots qu'ils sont imprenables. Shakespeare a un *Sunt lacrymæ rerum*. Dans le *We have kissed away kingdoms and provinces*, aussi bien que dans le profond soupir de Virgile, l'indicible est dit.

"Shakespeare échappe au traducteur par le style, il échappe aussi par la langue. L'anglais se dérobe le plus qu'il peut au français. Les deux idiomes sont composes en sens inverse. Leur pôle n'est pas le même: l'anglais est saxon, le français est latin.

Rien n'est plus laborieux que de faire coïncider ces deux idiomes. Ils semblent destinés à exprimer des choses opposées. L'un est septentrional, l'autre est méridional. L'un confine aux lieux cimmériens, aux bruyères, aux steppes, aux neiges, aux solitudes froides, aux espaces nocturnes, pleins de silhouettes indéterminées aux régions blèmes; l'autre confine aux régions claires. Il y a plus de lune dans celui-ci, et plus de soleil dans celui-là. Sud centre Nord, jour contre nuit, rayon contre spleen. Un nuage flotte toujours dans la phrase anglaise. Ce nuage est une beauté. Il est partout dans Shakespeare. Il faut que la clarté française pénètre ce nuage sans le dissoudre. Quelquefois la traduction doit se dilater," etc., etc.

"To translate him really, to translate him with confidence, to translate him in abandoning oneself to him, to translate him with honest simplicity noble in its enthusiasm, to elude nothing, to omit nothing, to weaken nothing, to conceal nothing, not to veil him here where he is naked, not to mask him there where he is sincere, not to take his skin from him beneath which to tell lies, to translate him without having recourse to circumlocution, this mental restriction, to translate him without a purist complaisance for France or a puritan one for England, to tell the truth, the whole truth, and nothing but the truth, to translate him as one gives testimony, not to betray him., to introduce him at Paris on equal terms, to take no insolent precautions for this genius, to propose to the mean of intelligences, which has the pretension to call itself taste, the acceptance of this giant: There he is! do you wish for him? not to cry beware, not to be ashamed of the great man, to avow him, to publish him far and wide, to proclaim him, to promulgate him, to be his flesh and his bones, to take his impress, to mould in his form, to think his thought, to speak his word, to make the French the echo of the English of Shakespeare,—what an enterprise!

"Shakespeare is one of the poets who defends himself the most against the translator.

He escapes by idea, he escapes by expression.

What intrepidity it requires to reproduce absolutely in French certain insolent beauties of this poet, for example, the 'buttock of the night,' where one has a glimpse of the shameful parts of darkness. Some other expressions seem without possible equivalents; thus 'green girl,' *fille verte*, has no sense in French. It could be said of certain expressions that they are impregnable. Shakespeare has a *Sunt lacrymæ rerum*. In the '*We have kissed away kingdoms and provinces*' as well as in the profound sigh of Virgil, the unutterable is said.

"Shakespeare escapes the translator by the style, he escapes also by the language. The English language withholds itself as much as it can from the French. The two idioms are composed in an inverse sense. Their pole is not the same: the English is Saxon, the French is Latin.

Nothing is more laborious than to make these two idioms coincide. They seem destined to express opposite things. One is northern, the other is southern. The one borders upon Cimmerian tracts, heaths, steppes, snows, cold solitudes, nocturnal spaces full of undefined outlines, pallid regions; the other borders upon bright regions. There is more of the moon in the one, and more of the sun in the other, south opposed to north, day against night, radiance against melancholy (*spleen*). A cloud always floats in the English phrase. This cloud is a beauty. It is everywhere in Shakespeare. It is necessary that French lucidity should penetrate this cloud without dissolving it. Sometimes the translation must extend itself," etc., etc.

All that is necessary in order to express my meaning completely is to substitute the names of "Victor Hugo" and "France," for "Shakespeare" and "England."

The reader will have here, I trust, the thoughts and opinions of the author in their integrity. He will understand the object he wished to attain; but his phosphorescent style, his images, which like beacons attract and fascinate the mind's eyes,—these he will not have. In spite of my best efforts, in spite of the zeal that I have brought to the work, he will have, I fear, but a mere skeleton of the brilliant original.

Duncombe Pyrke, junior.

Guernsey, *May*, 1865.

I cannot but be aware that the following letter is to be ascribed less to the justice of M. Victor Hugo than to his indulgent goodness. That he should recognize the zeal that I have brought to this work is all that I had the right to hope for; in going beyond this, he recompenses me more than I deserve.

If the letter of the illustrious writer was confined to this kind interpretation of my efforts, I should not perhaps publish it, but in it he touches in a few words the very bottom of the question, and I cannot pass over the least word or the smallest sentence on the subject proceeding from the pen of this great thinker. The following is the letter which I have received at the moment of going to press, and after having submitted my translation to M. Victor Hugo.

"Hauteville-House, 28 *mai*, 1865.

"Autant, Monsieur, que je puis juger d'une traduction anglaise, votre traduction de *Claude Gueux* est excellente.

"Vous avez, au plus haut degré, le soin littéraire et le sentiment délicat des devoirs d'un traducteur. Jusqu'à présent, un seul de mes livres, *William Shakespeare*, a été traduit avec cette intelligence et cette conscience. Je vous remercie et je vous félicite.

"La publication de *Claude Gueux* peut être de quelque utilité en Angleterre. Claude Gueux a existé, et le fait est réel. Au moment où la peine de mort est en question, à l'heure où se débattent devant l'opinion ces grands problèmes de la vie et de la mort, les plus grands de tous, votre traduction arrive à propos. Elle apporte une pièce au dossier. Vous faites là, Monsieur, un noble effort. Vous voulez populariser dans votre pays la haine de l'échafaud. Vous vous associez aux plus sérieuses tentatives sociales de ce siècle. Mon œuvre n'est rien, mais L'inviolabilité de la vie humaine, on peut presque le dire, est tout. Sans la vie humaine inviolable, pas de civilisation.

"Je vous renouvelle, Monsieur, l'expression de ma cordialité.

"Victor Hugo."

(*Translation.*)

"Hauteville House," 28th *May*, 1865.

"As far, sir, as I can judge of an English translation, your translation of 'Claude Gueux' is excellent.

"You have, in the highest degree, literary carefulness and a delicate sense of the duties of a translator. Up to the present time, one only of my books, 'William Shakespeare,' has been translated with this intelligence and this conscience. I thank you, and I congratulate you.

"The publication of 'Claude Gueux' may be of some utility in England. Claude Gueux existed, and the facts are real. At the moment in which the punishment of death is in question, at the time when in the presence of public opinion these great problems of life and death, the greatest of all, are agitated, your translation is opportune. It adds a document to the file. You make there, sir, a noble effort. You desire to popularize in your country the hatred of the scaffold. You associate yourself with the most important social efforts of this age. My work is nothing, but the inviolability of human life, it may almost be said, is everything. Without inviolable human life, there is no civilization.

"I renew to you, sir, the expression of my cordiality.

"Victor Hugo."

CLAUDE GUEUX.

Seven or eight years ago, [5] a man named Claude Gueux, a poor workman, lived at Paris. With him lived a young woman who was his mistress, and her child. I relate things as they are, leaving the reader to gather the moral lessons which the facts present on the way. The workman was capable, clever, intelligent, very badly treated by education, very well treated by nature, not knowing how to read and knowing how to think. One winter, work was not to be had. There was neither fire nor bread in the garret. The man, the girl, and the child were cold and hungry. The man committed a theft. I know not what he stole or where he stole; what I know is, that the result of this theft was three days' food and fire for the woman and child, and five years' imprisonment for the man.

[5] In 1834—*Tr.*

He was taken to the central establishment of Clairvaux, to undergo his sentence. Clairvaux, which was formerly an abbey, now converted into a bastile, where the monastic cell has been turned into a prison cell, and the altar into a pillory. When we speak of progress, it is thus that certain people comprehend it, and carry it into effect. That is what they place under our word.

Let us continue.

Arrived there, he was placed in a cell at night, and in a workshop by day. It is not the workshop that I blame.

Claude Gueux, an honest workman but lately, henceforth a thief, was of a grave and dignified appearance. He had a high forehead, already wrinkled though still young, amongst the black tufts a few grey hairs lay concealed, the eye was gentle and deeply sunken beneath a well formed and arched brow, the nostrils open, the chin prominent, the lip supercilious. It was a fine head. "We shall presently see what society did with it.

He seldom spoke, or used any gesture; there was something imperious in his whole person, which caused obedience, and he had a pensive air, as though serious rather than suffering. He had, however, suffered much.

In the depot where Claude was confined, there was a director of workshops, a sort of official peculiar to prisons, who partakes both of the turnkey and the tradesman, who at the same time deals out an order to the workman and a menace to the prisoner, who puts a tool in your hands and irons on your legs. This one was a variety of the species,—a man who was curt, tyrannical, obedient to his notions, always with a tight rein on his authority; otherwise, when the occasion offered itself, a boon companion, a jolly fellow, jovial even and jesting with grace; hard rather than firm; reasoning with no one, not even with himself; doubtless he was a good father, and a good husband, but that sort of goodness which is duty, and not virtue; in a word, not wicked, mischievous. He was one of those men who have nothing vibrating or elastic in their natures, who are composed of inert particles, in whom the shock of not one idea produces an echo, in contact with no sentiment, who have cold rages, sullen hatreds, passions without emotion, who catch fire without getting heated, whose capacity of caloric is none, and who, one would often say, are made of wood—they blaze at one end and are cold at the other. The principal feature (*la ligne principale la ligne diagonale*) of this man's character was tenacity. He was proud of being tenacious, and compared himself to Napoleon. This is but an optical illusion. There are many people who are its dupes, and who, at a certain distance, take tenacity for will and a candle for a star. When this man, therefore, had once adjusted what he called *his will* to an absurd thing, he went through with it with his head high and over every obstacle to the end of the absurd thing. Obstinacy without intelligence, is folly soldered on to stupidity and serving to prolong it. That goes a great way. Generally, when a private or public catastrophe has befallen us, if, after examining the ruins which strew the ground, we inquire how the building was put together, we find nearly always that it was blindly constructed by an inferior and stubborn man who had faith in and who admired himself. There are in the world a number of these little headstrong fatalities, who believe themselves to be providences.

Such, then, was the director of workshops of the central prison of Clairvaux. Such was the steel with which day after day society struck these prisoners and drew sparks from them.

The spark struck by such steel from such flint often blazes into a conflagration.

We have said that once arrived at Clairvaux, Claude Gueux was placed in a workshop, his name was changed into a number, and he was riveted to a labor. The director of the workshop made acquaintance with him, recognized him as a good workman, and treated him well. It appeared even that one day, being in a good humor, and seeing that Claude Gueux seemed very sad,—for this man was always thinking of her he called *his wife*,—he told him by way of joviality and diversion, and also to console him, that this unhappy creature had gone on the streets. Claude coldly asked him what had become of the child. It was not known.

At the end of some months, Claude became acclimatized to the air of the prison, and appeared no longer to mind about anything. A certain severe serenity, natural to his character, had resumed its ascendency.

At the end of the same space of time nearly, Claude had acquired a singular influence over all his companions. As if by a sort of tacit understanding, and without anyone, not even himself, knowing why, all these men consulted him, listened to him, admired him and imitated him, which is the last degree in the ascending scale of admiration. It was no trifling honor to be obeyed by all these rebellious natures. This empire came to him without his having thought of it. The expression of his eye had much to do with this. The eye of a man is a window through which one sees the thoughts which pass to and fro in his head.

Place a man who contains ideas amongst men who contain none, [6] at the end of a given time, by an irresistible law of attraction, all the tenebrous intellects will gravitate in humble adoration around the radiant intellect. There are some men who are iron, and others who are loadstone. Claude was loadstone.

[6] We give a literal translation of this metaphorical and vigorous expression, which compares the head of a man to a box, which contains or does not contain ideas.—*Tr.*

In less than three months, then, Claude had become the soul, the law, and the order of the workshop. As the hands on a dial, all these men moved around him. He must have doubted at times whether he was a king or a prisoner. He was a sort of pope, captive with his cardinals.

And, by a reaction altogether natural, the effect of which manifests itself in every degree, beloved by the prisoners, he was detested by the gaolers. It is always thus. Popularity is never unaccompanied by disfavor. The love of slaves is always doubled by the hatred of the masters.

Claude Gueux was a large eater. It was a peculiarity of his organization. He had a stomach of such a nature, that the food which was sufficient for two ordinary men barely sufficed him for the day. M. de Cotadilla had one of these appetites, and made a joke of it; but what is a laughing matter for a duke, a grandee of Spain, the possessor of five hundred thousand sheep, is a burden for a workman, and a misfortune for a prisoner.

Claude Gueux, at liberty in his garret, worked all day, earned his four-pound loaf, and ate it. Claude Gueux, in prison, worked all day and received invariably for his labor a pound and a half of bread and four ounces of meat. Prison allowance is inexorable. Claude, therefore, was habitually hungry in the prison of Clairvaux.

He was hungry, and that was all He did not speak of it; this was his nature.

One day, Claude had just devoured his meagre pittance, and had replaced himself at his loom, hoping to beguile hunger by work. The other prisoners ate cheerfully. One young man, pale, wan, and feeble, came and placed himself near him. He held in his hand his ration, which he had not yet touched, and a knife. He remained there standing up, near Claude, seemingly wishing to speak to him, and not daring to do so. This man, and his bread and meat, annoyed Claude.

"What dost thou want?" he said, at last, abruptly.

"That thou wilt render me a service," said the young man, timidly.

"What is it?" replied Claude.

"That thou wilt help me to eat this; I have too much."

A tear glistened in Claude's proud eye. He took the knife, divided the young man's ration into two equal parts, took one of them, and set to eating.

"Thanks," said the young man. "If thou wilt, we will share like that every day."

"What is thy name?" said Claude Gueux.

"Albin."

"Why art thou here?" returned Claude.

"For stealing."

"And I, also," said Claude.

And, in fact, they continued to share like this every day. Claude Gueux was thirty-six years of age, and at times he seemed fifty, so intense was his constant habit of thought. Albin was twenty; one would have put him at seventeen, so much innocence was there still in the look of this thief. A close friendship united these two men, the friendship of father and son rather than that of brother and brother. Albin was still almost a child, Claude was already almost an old man.

They worked in the same workshop, they slept under the same keystone, they walked in the same yard, they ate of the same loaf. Each of these two friends was all the world for the other. It seemed that they were happy.

We have already spoken of the director of the workshops. This man, hated by the prisoners, was often obliged, to make himself obeyed by them, to have recourse to Claude Gueux, who was beloved by them. On more than one occasion, when the prevention of a rebellion or a tumult was in question, the unsanctioned authority of Claude Gueux lent a strong arm to the official authority of the director. In fact, to restrain the prisoners, ten words of Claude Gueux were worth ten gendarmes. Claude had several times rendered this service to the director. Consequently the director detested him cordially. He was jealous of this thief. He had at the bottom of his heart, a secret, envious, implacable hatred against Claude, the hatred that a rightful sovereign has to the actual sovereign, that temporal power has to spiritual power.

These hatreds are the worst.

Claude loved Albin much, and never thought of the director.

One day, in the morning, at the time when the turnkeys transferred the prisoners two by two from the dormitory to the workshop, a turnkey called Albin, who was at the side of Claude, and informed him that the director wanted him.

"What do they want thee for?" said Claude.

"I do not know," said Albin.

The turnkey led away Albin.

The morning passed away, and Albin did not return to the workshop. When the dinner hour came, Claude thought that he should find Albin in the yard again. Albin was not in the yard. They returned to the workshop. Albin had not reappeared in the workshop. Thus the day passed away. In the evening, when they took the prisoners back to the dormitory, Claude sought with his eyes for Albin, but did not see him. He must have suffered much at that moment, for he addressed a turnkey,—a thing that he never did.

"Is Albin ill?" said he.

"No," answered the turnkey.

"What is the reason, then," returned Claude, "that he has not reappeared today?"

"Ah!" said the turnkey, carelessly, "it is because they have changed his ward."

Witnesses who have since deposed to these facts, remarked that on receiving this answer from the turnkey, Claude's hand, in which was a lighted candle, trembled slightly. He returned, with calmness,—

"Who gave that order?"

The turnkey answered,—

"Monsieur D."

This was the name of the director of workshops.

The following day passed like the preceding one, without Albin.

In the evening, at the time they left off work Monsieur D. came to make his habitual round in the workshop. As soon as Claude caught sight of him, he doffed his coarse woollen cap, buttoned his grey waistcoat, the sombre livery of Clairvaux, for it is a maxim in prisons that a waistcoat respectfully buttoned makes a favorable impression on the superiors, and stood up with his cap in his hand, at the end of his bench, waiting for the director to pass. The director passed.

"Sir!" said Claude.

The director stopped, and turned himself half round.

"Sir," continued Claude, "is it true that Albin's ward has been changed?"

"Yes," answered the director.

"Sir," said Claude, "I have need of Albin that I may live."

He added,—

"You know that I have not enough to eat with the prison allowance, and that Albin shared his bread with me."

"That was his business," said the director.

"Sir, cannot Albin be put back into the same ward with me?"

"Impossible. It has been decided."

"By whom?"

"By me."

"Monsieur D.," returned Claude, "it is life or death for me, and it depends on you."

"I never alter my decisions."

"Sir, have I done anything to displease you?"

"Nothing."

"In that case," said Claude, "why do you separate me from Albin?"

"Because" (*parce que*), [7] said the director. This explanation given, the director passed out.

[7] This word, which is the *ultima ratio* with people who have no good reason to give for their conduct, will be understood by those of our readers who know the French language. It is almost proverbial in this sense. It is the last word with angry and obstinate women. It will be seen that this word was repeated by *Claude Gueux* when under examination, thus recalling the fact that the director had made use of it to express his unchangeable determination, for which he did not choose to give any reason.—*Tr.*

Claude drooped his head, and did not reply. Poor caged lion, whom they had deprived of his dog!

We are bound to say that the grief of this separation altered in no way the sort of morbid voracity possessed by the prisoner. Nothing besides seemed sensibly changed in him. He did not speak of Albin to any of his comrades. He walked alone in the yard in the hours of recreation, and he was hungry. Nothing more.

However, those who knew him well, remarked something sinister and gloomy in his countenance, which grew more and more lowering every day. Otherwise, he was more gentle than ever.

Many wished to share their ration with him; he refused, with a smile.

Every evening, since the explanation which the director had given to him, he did a silly sort of thing that was surprising in a man of so serious a disposition. At the time that the director returned to make his usual round, at the hour fixed for that duty, as he passed before Claude's loom, Claude raised his eyes and looked at him fixedly; then he addressed to him, in a tone full of anguish and rage, which at the same time partook of the prayer and the menace, these two words only, "And Albin?" (*Et Albin?*) The director pretended not to hear him, or passed on with a shrug of the shoulders.

This man was wrong to shrug his shoulders, for it was evident to all the spectators of these strange scenes that Claude Gueux had inwardly determined on something. All the prison awaited with anxiety the result of this struggle between tenacity and resolution.

It has been proved that upon one occasion, amongst others, Claude said to the director,—

"Listen, sir. Give me back my comrade. You will do well, I assure you. Observe, that I tell you so."

Another time, on a Sunday, he was in the yard, seated on a stone, his elbows on his knees and his face in his hands, where he remained motionless in the same attitude for several hours, when the convict Faillette came towards him, and exclaimed, laughing,—

"What the deuce art thou doing there, Claude?"

Claude slowly raised his severe-looking head, and said,—

"*I am sitting in judgment upon someone*" (*je juge quelqu'un*).

One evening, at last, the 25th of October, 1831, whilst the director was making his round, Claude crushed with his foot a watch-glass which he had found that morning in the corridor. The director asked from whence came the noise.

"It is nothing," said Claude, "it is I. Monsieur le Directeur, give me back my comrade."

"Impossible," said the master.

"It must be done, however," said Claude, in a low, firm voice. And, looking the director in the face, he added,—

"Reflect. Today is the 25th of October; I give you till the 4th of November."

A turnkey remarked to Monsieur D. that Claude threatened him, and that it was a case for the dark cell.

"No,—no dark cell," said the director, with a scornful smile. "One must be lenient with these sort of people!"

The next day the convict Pernot came up to Claude, who was walking about alone and pensive, leaving the other prisoners to enjoy themselves in a little square of sun at the other end of the court.

"Well, Claude, what art thou thinking about? Thou seemest sad."

"*I am afraid*" said Claude, "*that some misfortune will soon befall this good Monsieur D.*"

There are nine clear days from the 25th of October to the 4th of November. Claude did not let one of them pass without gravely informing the director of the affliction, which was becoming more and more grievous, that the disappearance of Albin caused him. The director, wearied out, once inflicted on him twenty-four hours of the dark cell, because the petition bore too strong a resemblance to a summons. This was all Claude obtained.

The 4th of November arrived. That day Claude awoke with a serene countenance, the like of which had not been seen in him since the day when the decision of Monsieur D. had separated him from his friend. On getting up, he searched in a sort of chest of white wood, which was at the foot of his bed, and which contained his few rags. He took out of it a pair of scissors, such as seamstresses use. With an odd volume of 'Emile,' it was the only thing which remained to him of the woman he had loved, of the mother of his child, of his happy little household of former time. Two very useless articles for Claude: the scissors could be of use only to a woman, the book only to a person of education. Claude knew neither how to sew nor how to read.

As Claude traversed the venerable and desecrated cloister, covered with whitewash, which serves as a place to walk in during the winter, he went up to the convict Ferrari, who was looking with attention at the enormous bars of one of the windows. Claude held in his hand the little pair of scissors; he showed them to Ferrari, and said,—

"This evening I shall cut through those bare with this pair of scissors."

Ferrari, unbelieving, burst out laughing, and Claude also.

On that morning he worked with more ardor than usual; never before had he worked so quickly and so well. He seemed to attach a certain importance upon finishing on that morning a straw hat for which he had been paid in advance by a worthy citizen of Troyes, M. Bressier.

A little before twelve o'clock he made some pretext for going down to the joiners' workshop, situated on the ground floor, which was below the one in which he worked. Claude was beloved there as elsewhere, but he rarely entered it. Therefore,—

"See! there is Claude!"

They surrounded him. It was an ovation. Claude cast a rapid glance round the room. None of the warders were there.

"Who has got an axe to lend me?" said he.

"What for?" they asked him.

He answered,—

"To kill the director of workshops with, this evening."

Several axes were offered him to choose from. He took the smallest, which was very sharp, hid it in his trousers, and went away.

There were there twenty-seven prisoners. He did not enjoin secrecy. All observed it.

They did not even talk upon the subject amongst themselves.

Each on his part awaited with anxiety the event which was about to happen. It was a terrible affair, simple and definite. There could be no possible complication. Claude could neither be advised nor denounced.

One hour later, he approached a young man who was yawning in the corridor, and advised him to learn to read.

At this moment, the prisoner Faillette accosted Claude, and asked him what the deuce he had concealed in his trousers.

Claude said,—

"It is an axe, with which to kill Monsieur D. this evening." He added,—

"Does it show?"

"A little," said Faillette.

The rest of the day passed in the ordinary manner. At seven o'clock in the evening, they shut up the prisoners, each section in the workshop which was assigned to it; and the warders left the labor-wards, as it appeared was their custom, not to return until after the director's round.

Claude Gueux was then locked up, like the rest, in his workshop, with those who worked at the same trade as himself.

Then there occurred in that workshop an extraordinary scene,—a scene that is not without grandeur, nor without horror, the only one of its kind that any history can relate.

There were there, according to the judicial examination which afterwards took place, eighty-two thieves, including Claude.

As soon as the warders had left them alone, Claude stood up on his bench, and announced to the whole company that he had something to say. There was silence.

Then Claude raised his voice, and said,—

"All of you know that Albin was a brother to me. I have not enough to eat with what they give me here. Even in spending the little that I earn on bread alone, I should not have enough. Albin shared his ration with me; I loved him at first because he fed me, and afterwards because he loved me. The director, Monsieur D., has separated us, not that it mattered to him that we were together; but he is a wicked man, who delights in tormenting. I have asked for Albin back again. As you have seen, he has not chosen to comply. I have given him till the 4th of November to restore Albin to me. He has sent me to the dark cell for having said that. I, during that time, have judged him, and I have condemned him to death; [8] the 4th of November has arrived. In two hours he will come to make his round. I inform you that I am going to kill him. Have you anything to say to that?"

[8] Textual.

All kept silence.

Claude resumed. He spoke, as it seemed, with a singular eloquence, which moreover was natural to him. He declared that he knew well that he was going to commit a deed of violence, but that he did not believe himself to be wrong.

He called to witness the conscience of the eighty-one thieves who heard him,—

That he was in a painful extremity;

That the necessity of taking the law into one's own hands was a difficulty in which one is sometimes placed;

That in truth he could not take the director's life without giving his own, but that he thought it good to give his life for a thing that was just;

That he had maturely reflected on the subject, and on that only, for two months past;

That he believed it right not to allow himself to be carried away by resentment, but if that should be the case, he begged that they would warn him of it;

That he honestly submitted his conclusions to the just men who heard him;

That he should proceed therefore to kill Monsieur D., but that if anyone had any objection to make, he was ready to hear him.

One voice only raised itself, and said that before killing the director, Claude should try a last time to speak to him and to move him.

"It is right," said Claude, "and I will do it."

The great clock struck eight. The director was to come at nine.

When once this strange court of appeal had in a certain manner ratified the sentence that he had pronounced, Claude resumed all his serenity. He placed on a table all that he possessed in the way of linen and clothing, the poor effects of a prisoner, and calling up one after the other those of his companions he loved the best after Albin, he distributed all amongst them. He only kept the small pair of scissors.

Then he embraced all of them. Some wept; to these he gave a smile.

There were, in this last hour, some moments when he conversed with so much tranquility, and even cheerfulness, that many of his comrades entertained a secret hope, as they have since declared, that lie would perhaps abandon his resolution. Once even he amused himself by extinguishing one of the few candles which lighted the workshop by blowing it out with his nostrils; for he had some bad habits of education which detracted from his natural dignity more frequently than should have been the case. Nothing could prevent this *ancien gamin* of the streets from having about him at times the odor of the Paris kennels.

He observed a young convict who was pale, who looked at him with fixed eyes, and who trembled, no doubt at the anticipation of what he was going to see.

"Come, courage, young man!" said Claude, softly, to him, "it will only be the affair of a moment."

When he had distributed all his clothes, bid farewell to everybody, and shaken hands all round, he interrupted some restless conversation that was going on here and there in the obscure corners of the workshop, and ordered work to be resumed. All obeyed, in silence.

The workshop where this took place was an oblong room, a long parallelogram pierced with windows on the two principal sides, and with two doors placed opposite one another at its two extremities. The looms were arranged on each side near the windows, the benches touching the walls at right angles, and the space that was left between the two rows of looms formed a sort of long pathway which went in a straight line from one of the two doors to the other, and consequently crossed the entire length of the room. It was down this long pathway, which was narrow enough, that the director had to pass in making his inspection; he would enter by the south door and leave by the north door, after having looked at those at work on his right-hand and on his left. Ordinarily, he made this passage rather quickly, and without stopping.

Claude replaced himself on his bench, and resumed his work, as Jacques Clément resumed his prayer. [9]

[9] Most of our readers will recollect, probably, that Jacques Clément was a young fanatical monk, who was sent from Paris by the chiefs of the League, and notably by the Duchesse de Montpensier, to assassinate the King, Henri III.

When Jacques Clément arrived at the Palace of St. Cloud, after having demanded an audience of the King, he awaited the arrival of this prince in the audience-chamber, and knelt down in prayer in the midst of the courtiers who passed to and fro around him, When the King arrived, Jacques Clément knelt down before him, presented him with a writing of which he was the bearer, and, while his Majesty was perusing it, stabbed him in the abdomen with a long knife; ho then with calmness resumed the prayer be had commenced on entering.—*Tr.*

Claude replaced himself on his bench, and resumed his work, as Jacques Clément resumed his prayer.

All waited in expectation. The moment approached. All at once the clock was heard to strike. Claude said,—

"It is the quarter before."

Then he arose, traversed gravely a part of the room, and went and leaned on his elbow upon a corner of the first loom on the left, next to the door of entrance. His countenance was perfectly calm and benignant. Nine o'clock struck. The door opened,—the director entered.

At that moment, in the workshop, there was a silence of statues.

The director was alone, as usual.

He entered with his jaunty, self-satisfied, and inexorable manner,—did not see Claude, who was standing up on the left of the door, with his right hand concealed in his trousers,—and passed rapidly before the first looms, shaking his head, mincing his words, and casting here and there his vague everyday look, without perceiving that all the eyes around him were fixed upon some terrible idea.

Suddenly he turned round sharply, surprised at hearing a footstep behind him.

It was Claude, who had followed him in silence for some moments.

"What art thou doing there?" said the director; "why art thou not in thy place?" For a man is no longer a man there; he is a dog; they thee and thou him.

Claude Gueux answered, respectfully,—

"I want to speak to you, Monsieur le Directeur."

"About what?"

"About Albin."

"Again!" said the director.

"Always!" said Claude.

"Come!" replied the director, walking on, "twenty-four hours of the dark cell has not been enough for thee?"

Claude answered, continuing to follow him,—

"Monsieur le Directeur, give me back my comrade."

"Impossible!"

"Monsieur le Directeur," said Claude, in a tone which would have softened the demon, "I beseech you, put Albin back with me; you will see how well I shall work. You who are free, it is the same thing to you, you do not know what a friend is; but as for me,

I have only the four walls of the prison. You—you can come and go; as for me, I have only Albin. Give him back to me. Albin supplied me with food,—you know it well. It would only cost you the trouble of saying Yes. What is it to you that there should be in the same room one man named Claude Gueux, and another named Albin? For it is not more complicated than that Monsieur le Directeur, my good Monsieur D., I beseech you, indeed, in the name of heaven!"

Claude had perhaps never before said so much at a time to a gaoler. After this effort, exhausted, he waited. The director replied, with a gesture of impatience,—

"Impossible. It is said. Look here, do not speak to me about it any more; thou weariest me."

And, as he was in a hurry, he hastened on; Claude also. Speaking in this manner, they arrived both together close to the door of exit,—the eighty thieves looked on and listened, breathless.

Claude touched softly the director's arm.

"But, at least, let me know why I am condemned to death. Tell me why you have separated him from me?"

"I have already told thee," answered the director. "Because." (*Parce que*.)

And, turning his back upon Claude, he advanced his hand towards the handle of the door of exit.

At the answer of the director, Claude fell back a pace. The eighty statues there present saw his right hand quit his trousers, with the axe in it. This hand rose, and, before the director could utter a cry, three blows of the axe, frightful thing to relate, all three aimed at and delivered on the same spot, had laid open his skull. At the moment that he tumbled backwards, a fourth blow gashed his face; then, as rage once set going never stops short, Claude Gueux cleaved open his right thigh with a fifth and useless blow. The director was dead.

Then Claude threw away the axe and cried out,—"*Now for the other!*"

The other was himself. He was seen to take from his waistcoat the small pair of scissors that had belonged to his "wife;" and, before anyone had thought of preventing him, he plunged them in his breast. The blade was short, his breast was deep. He worked it about there a long time, plunging it in again and again, more than twenty times, crying out, "Heart of the accursed, shall I not then find thee!" and, at length, bathed in his blood, he fell upon the corpse, senseless.

Which of the two was the victim of the other?

When Claude came to his senses, he was in a bed covered with linen and bandages, surrounded with care and attention. There were near the head of his bed some good Sisters of Charity, and besides, a *juge d'instruction* who was drawing up a legal document, and who asked him, with much interest,—

"*How do you find yourself?*"

He had lost a great quantity of blood, but the scissors with which he had had the touching superstition to strike himself, had badly performed their duty: none of the injuries he had given himself were dangerous. His only mortal wounds were those he had dealt Monsieur D.

The examinations commenced. He was asked if it was he who had killed the director of the workshops of Clairvaux. He answered,—

"*Yes.*"

He was asked why. He answered,—

"Because." [10] (*Parce que*.)

[10] See note, page 15.

In the meanwhile, at a certain time, his wounds festered; he was taken with a bad fever, of which he nearly died.

November, December, January, and February, passed away in attentions and preparations; doctors and judges vied with each about Claude: some of them cured his wounds, the others erected his scaffold.

Let us be brief. On the 16th of March, 1832, he appeared, being perfectly recovered, before the Court of Assizes of Troyes. All the crowd that the town could furnish was there.

Claude made a good appearance before the court. He was shaved with care, he had his head bare, and he wore that dismal costume of the prisoners of Clairvaux, which is half one sort of grey and half another.

The King's Procureur had choked up the hall with all the bayonets of the arrondissement, "in order," as he said to the court, "to keep in all the scoundrels who were to figure as witnesses in that affair."

When they were about to enter upon the proceedings, a singular difficulty presented itself: none of the witnesses of the events of the 4th of November would give evidence against Claude. The president threatened them with his discretionary power; it was in vain. Claude then ordered them to give evidence. All the tongues were unloosed: they related what they had seen.

Claude listened to them with a profound attention. When one of them, through forgetfulness or through affection for Claude, omitted some facts charged against the prisoner, Claude set him right.

From testimony to testimony, the series of facts we have set forth unrolled itself before the court.

There was one moment when all the women who were present wept. The usher called the convict Albin. It was his turn to give evidence. He entered trembling; he sobbed. The gendarmes could not prevent him from rushing into the arms of Claude. Claude supported him, and said to the King's Procureur, with a smile,—

"See, there is a reprobate who shares his bread with the hungry." Then he kissed Albin's hand.

The list of witnesses exhausted, the King's Procureur arose, and spoke in these terms,—

"Gentlemen of the jury, society would be shaken to its foundations if public vengeance did not overtake great culprits like him who," etc.

After this memorable speech, Claude's advocate spoke. The pleading for and pleading against made, each in their turn, the evolutions that they are accustomed to make in that sort of exhibition known as a criminal trial.

Claude considered that all had not been said. He arose, in his turn. He spoke in such a manner that a person who was present at this trial returned from it struck with astonishment.

It seemed that this poor workman was much more of an orator than an assassin. He spoke standing up, with a penetrating and well-managed voice, with a bright, honest, and resolute eye, with a gesture nearly always the same, but full of command. He spoke of things as they were simply, seriously, without changing or extenuating anything, confessed everything, looked Article 296 [11] in the face, and placed his head beneath.

There were some moments when he spoke with a real lofty eloquence which caused the crowd to stir, and when what he had just said was repeated amongst them in a whisper.

[11] Article 296 is the article of the *Code Pénal* which has reference to murder committed with premeditation, and which carries with it the punishment of death. It will be understood that Article 296 is here compared to the executioner's axe, and that to look this article in the face is to brave this axe, and in a certain manner to put the head beneath it, as the author says in a fine image.—*Tr*.

This caused a murmur, during which Claude drew breath, casting a proud look upon those present.

At other times this man, who knew not how to read, was as gentle, polished, choice in expression as an educated person; then, some moments again, he was modest, circumspect, attentive, moving step by step at the irritating part of the inquiry, paying deference to the judges.

Once only he allowed himself to get into a passion. The King's Procureur had laid down, in the speech that we have cited in its entirety, that Claude Gueux had assassinated the director of the workshops without blows or violence on the part of the director, consequently *without provocation.*

"What!" cried Claude, "I have not been provoked! Ah, yes, truly it is right! I understand you. A drunken man gives me a blow with his fist; I kill him; I have been provoked, you pardon me, you send me to the galleys. But a man who is not drunk, and who has all his reason, crushes my heart for four years, humiliates me for four years, goads me every day, every hour, every minute, somewhere unexpectedly as with the thrust of a pin, for four years! I had a wife for whom I robbed; he tortures me with this wife. I had a child for whom I robbed; he tortures me with this child. I have not enough bread; a friend gives me some, he takes away my friend and my bread. I ask for my friend back, he sends me to the dark cell. I say to him—to him, a spy—*you*, he says to me *thou*. I tell him I suffer, he tells me that I weary him. Then what would you have me do? I kill him. It is well, I am a monster,—I have killed that man,—I have not been provoked,—you cut off my head for me. Do it."

A sublime impulse, in our opinion, which caused an entire theory of moral provocation, forgotten by the law, all at once to rise above the system of material provocation, upon which rests the badly proportioned scale of attenuating circumstances.

The case being closed, the president made his impartial and luminous summing up. There resulted from it this: a shameful life,—in fact, a monster. Claude Gueux had commenced by living in concubinage with a girl of the town; then he had committed robbery; then murder. All that was true.

As the jurymen were about to be sent to their apartment, the president asked the accused if he had anything to say with reference to the placing of the questions.

"Very little," said Claude. "This, however. I am a thief and an assassin. I have robbed and I have killed. But why have I robbed? Why did I kill? Place these two questions by the side of the others, gentlemen of the jury."

After a quarter of an hour's deliberation, upon the finding of the twelve Champenois [12] who were called the gentlemen of the jury, Claude was condemned to death.

[12] *Douze Champenois*. We do not know whether the author, in designating the jurymen by the name of their province, had the ironical intention of recalling to the reader the French proverb: *Quatre-vingt-dix-neuf moutons et un Champenois font cent bêtes.*

It is certain that, since the opening of the proceedings, many amongst them had remarked that the accused was named Gueux, [13] which made a profound impression on them.

[13] *Gueux*. A word which in the French language expresses two very different ideas. *Gueux* means a poor man, without money, etc.; it means, also, a vagabond, a worthless fellow.—*Tr.*

The sentence was read to Claude, who contented himself with saying,—
"*It is well. But why has this man robbed? Why has this man committed murder? There are two questions which they do not answer.*"
Having re-entered the prison, he ate his supper cheerfully and said,—
"Thirty-six years of facts!"
He did not wish to appeal. One of the Sisters who had taken care of him came and besought him to do so with tears. He appealed, out of complaisance for her. It appeared that he resisted to the very last instant, for, at the moment that he signed his appeal on the register of the *greffe*, the legal delay of three days had expired by some minutes.
The poor girl, grateful, gave him five francs. He took the money, and thanked her.
Whilst his application was pending; some offers of escape were made to him by the prisoners of Troyes, who all were ready to devote themselves to it. He refused.
The prisoners threw successively into his dungeon, by the air-hole, a nail, a bit of iron wire, and a bucket handle. Anyone of these three tools would have sufficed for a man as intelligent as Claude was, wherewith to file through his irons. He gave up the handle, the iron wire, and the nail, to the turnkey.
On the 8th of June, 1832, seven months and four days after the deed, the expiation came, *pede claudo*, as it seemed. On this day, at seven o'clock in the morning, the greffier of the court entered Claude's dungeon, and announced to him that he had but one more hour to live.
His appeal was rejected.
"Come along," said Claude, coolly. "I have slept well this night, without doubting that I should sleep still better the next."
It appears that the words of strong men always acquire at the approach of death a certain greatness.
The priest arrived, then the executioner. He was humble with the priest, and gentle with the other. He refused neither his soul nor his body.
He preserved a perfect freedom of mind. Whilst they were cutting off his hair, someone spoke, in a corner of the cell, of the cholera which threatened Troyes at that moment.
"As for me," said Claude, with a smile, "I have no fear of the cholera."
He listened, moreover, to the priest with the greatest attention, at the same time reproaching himself much, and regretting not to have been instructed in religion.
At his request, they had given him back the scissors with which he had struck himself. One of the blades was wanting, which had broken in his breast. He desired the gaoler to cause these scissors to be given to Albin from him. He said, also, that he desired

that there should be added to this legacy the ration of bread that he would have eaten on that day.

He requested those who tied his hands to put in his right hand the five-franc piece that the Sister had given him,—the only thing that remained to him from this time forth.

At a quarter to eight o'clock he left the prison, with all the ordinary lugubrious *cortége* of condemned criminals. He was on foot, pale, with his eye fixed on the priest's crucifix, but walking with a firm step.

They had chosen that day for the execution, because it was the market-day, in order that as many as possible should see him pass; for it seems that there are yet in France some small, half-savage borough towns, where, when society kills a man, it makes a boast of it.

He mounted the scaffold gravely, keeping his eye fixed on the gibbet of Christ. He wished to embrace the priest, then the executioner,—thanking the one, forgiving the other. The executioner *repulsed him gently*, one account said. As the assistant was tying him upon the hideous piece of mechanism, he made a sign to the priest to take the five-franc piece that he had in his right hand, and said to him,—

"*For the poor.*"

As eight o'clock struck just at that moment, the noise of the clock bell drowned his voice, and the confessor answered that he did not hear. Claude waited the interval of two strokes, and repeated, meekly,—

"*For the poor.*"

The eighth stroke had not yet struck when this noble and intelligent head fell.

Admirable effect of public executions! That same day, while the machine was still standing in the midst of them, and not cleaned, there was an outbreak of the market-people on a question of tariff, and they all but murdered an officer of the *octroi* [14]—the gentle people who make those laws for you!

[14] The municipal tax levied on articles of consumption in all French towns.—*Tr.*

We believed it our duty to relate the story of Claude Gueux in detail, because, in our opinion, each paragraph of this history would serve as the head of a chapter in the book in which should be resolved the great problem of the people of the nineteenth century.

In this important life there are two principal phases,—before the fall, after the fall; and, under these two phases, two questions,—the question of education, the question of punishment; and, between these two questions, society in its entirety.

This man, certainly, was well born, well organized, well endowed. What was there wanting in him, then? Reflect.

Therein lies the great problem of proportion, the solution of which, still to be found, will bring to pass universal equilibrium: *That society should always do as much for the individual as nature does.*

See Claude Gueux. He had a well-formed brain and a good heart, without any doubt. But fate places him in a society so badly constituted that he ends by stealing; society places him in a prison so badly constituted that he ends by killing.

Who is really to blame? Is he? Are we?

These are severe questions, poignant questions, which claim at this time the attention of all intelligent minds, which pluck us all, everyone of us, by the skirt, and which will one day so completely bar our road, that it would be well to look them in the face and know what they demand of us.

He who writes these lines will try to say soon, perhaps, in what manner he understands them.

When in presence of such facts, when we think of the urgency of these questions, we ask what are those who govern us thinking of, if not of them?

The Chambers, every year, are seriously occupied. It is, no doubt, very important to reduce sinecures and to clear the budget; it is very important to make laws in order that I may go, disguised as a soldier, patriotically to mount guard at the gate of M. le Comte de Lobau, whom I do not know and whom I do not care to know, or to oblige me to parade in Marigny Square at the good pleasure of my grocer, who has been made my officer. [15]

[15] It is hardly necessary to say that we have no intention here of attacking the city patrol, a useful thing, which guards the street, the threshold, and the fireside, but only ornament, parade, ostentation, and military fuss,—absurdities which serve only to make a citizen the parody of a soldier.

It is important, for deputies or ministers, to worry and pull about everything and every idea of this country in discussions full of abortions; it is essential, for instance, to place at the bar, and to interrogate and to examine with loud cries, and without knowing what one says, the science of the nineteenth century, this great and severe culprit who does not deign to reply, and who does well; it is expedient for those who govern and those who legislate, to pass their time in classical discussions which make district schoolmasters shrug their shoulders; it is useful to declare that it is the modern drama which has invented incest, adultery, parricide, infanticide, and poisoning, and to prove from that that no one knows Phèdre, or Jocaste, or Œdipe, or Médée, or Rodogune; it is indispensable that the political orators of this country should wrangle for three long days, *à propos* of the budget, for Corneille and Racine, against no one knows who, and that they should profit by this literary occasion to vie with one another in plunging up to the very hilt into the gorge of great faults in French.

All that is important. We believe, nevertheless, that it is possible for there to be things still more important.

"What would the Chamber say, in the middle of the futile disputes which so often cause the Opposition to collar the ministry and the ministry the Opposition, if suddenly from the seats of the Chamber or the public tribune, what does it matter? someone should arise and utter these weighty words,—

"Be silent, whoever you may be, you who speak here, be silent! You think you know what the question is; you do not.

"The question is this: Justice, scarcely a year ago, mangled a man at Pamiers with a common knife; at Dijon she tore off a woman's head; at Paris she holds at the Barrière Saint-Jacques unpublished executions.

"This is the question. Occupy yourselves with this.

"You can quarrel amongst yourselves afterwards to know if the buttons of the National Guard ought to be white or yellow, and if *assurance* is a finer thing than *certitude*.

"Gentlemen of the centres, gentlemen of the extremities, the mass of the people suffer. Whether you call them republic or monarchy, the people suffer. This is a fact.

"The people are hungry; the people are cold. Misery drives them to crime or to vice, according to the sex. Have pity for the people, of whose sons and whose daughters the bagnio and the brothel take possession. You have too many galley slaves, you have too many prostitutes.

"What do these two ulcers prove?

"That the social body has a vice in the blood.

"There you are united in consultation at the sick man's bedside; occupy yourselves with the disease.

"You treat this disease badly. Study it better. The laws that you make, when you make them, are only palliatives and expedients. One half of your codes is routine, the other half empiricism.

"Branding was a cauterization which caused the wound to gangrene; a senseless punishment which for life sealed and riveted the crime on the criminal, which made of them two friends, two companions, two inseparables.

"The bagnio is an irrational blister which allows to be reabsorbed, not without having made it still worse, almost all the bad blood it extracts. The punishment of death is a barbarous amputation.

"Now, branding, the bagnio, capital punishment, are three things which are closely related. You have suppressed branding; if you are logical, suppress the rest.

"The branding-iron, the ball, [16] and the executioner's knife, were the three parts of a syllogism.

[16] That is, the cannon ball, which is or used to be attached by a chain to the convict's leg.—*Tr.*

"You have abolished the branding-iron; the ball and the executioner's knife have no longer any sense. Farinace was atrocious, but he was not absurd.

"Abolish this old halting scale of crimes and punishments, and remodel it. Remodel your punishment, remodel your codes, remodel your prisons, remodel your judges. Replace the laws on a footing with morality.

"Gentlemen, there are too many heads cut off in France every year. Since you are in the humor to make economies, make one upon that.

"Since you are in the mood for suppressions, suppress the executioner. With the pay of your eighty executioners you could pay six hundred schoolmasters.

"Think of the mass of the people. Let us have schools for the children, workshops for the men.

"Are you aware that France is one of the countries in Europe where there are the smallest number of natives who know how to read? What! Switzerland can read, Belgium can read, Denmark can read, Greece can read, Ireland can read, and France cannot read! It is a disgrace.

"Go into the bagnios. Call around you the whole crew. Examine one by one all these men damned by human law. Calculate the inclination of all these profiles; feel all these skulls. Each of these fallen men has beneath him his bestial type; it seems as if each of them is the point of intersection of humanity between such or such an animal species. Here is the lynx, here the cat, here the ape, here the vulture, here the hyena. Now, for these poor badly formed heads, the first wrong belongs to nature, doubtless; the second to education.

"Nature has made the rough draft badly, education has badly retouched the rough draught. Turn your attention to this. A good education for the people. Develop in the best way you can these unhappy heads, in order that the intelligence which is within may be able to grow.

"Nations have the skull well or ill formed, according to their institutions.

"Rome and Greece had the high forehead. Open as much as you can the facial angle of the people.

"When France knows how to read, do not leave without direction this intelligence that you will have developed. That would be another disorder. Ignorance is still better than bad knowledge. No. Recollect that there is a book more philosophic than the 'Compère Mathieu,' more popular than the 'Constitutionnel,' more eternal than the Charter of 1830. It is the Holy Scripture. And here, a word of explanation.

"Whatever you do, the lot of the great crowd, of the multitude, of the *majority*, will be always relatively poor, miserable, and sad. For it hard toil, burdens to urge forward, burdens to drag, burdens to bear.

"Examine this pair of scales,—all the enjoyments in the scale of the rich, all the miseries in the scale of the poor. The two parts, are they not unequal? Must not the scale necessarily lean over, and the State with it?

"And now in the lot of the poor, in the scale of the miserable, throw in the certainty of a heavenly future, throw in the aspiration for eternal happiness, throw in paradise. Magnificent counterpoise! You re-establish the equilibrium. The part of the poor is as rich as that of the rich.

"This is what Jesus knew, who knew it better than Voltaire.

"Give to the people who toil and who suffer, give to the people for whom this world is evil, the belief in a better world prepared for them.

"They will be tranquil; they will be patient Patience is made of hope.

"Sow, then, the villages with Gospels. A Bible for every cottage. Let every book and every field produce its moral laborer.

"The head of the man of the people,—that is the question. That head is full of useful germs. Treat it so that it may come to maturity, and bring forth that which is most enlightened and temperate in virtue.

"Many a one has assassinated on the high-roads, who, better directed, would have been a most excellent citizen.

"Cultivate this head of the man of the people; clear it, water it, fertilize it, enlighten it, moralize it, make it useful. You will have no need to cut it off."

THE END OF CLAUDE GUEUX.

THE LAST DAY OF A CONDEMNED MAN.

PREFACE.

At the head of the first editions of tibia work, then published without the author's name, the following lines only were written,—

"There are two ways of accounting for the existence of this book: either there was discovered a package of time-stained fragments of paper upon which were registered the last thoughts of an unhappy wretch; or, a man stepped forth, a dreamer—occupied in the study of nature that art may progress—a philosopher, a poet, I may not divine which; in fact, one in whom this idea was the leading fancy,—who, grasping it, or rather being carried away by it, could only rid himself of it by putting it into a book. Of these two explanations the reader may choose the one which best pleases him."

As may be seen, at the period in which the book was first given to the public, the author did not think fit to express his idea fully. He preferred waiting until it was more developed in the public mind, and to watch this development. It has been understood. The author can, at this present time, reveal the idea—both in its political and social aspects—which he desired to popularize under this frank and simple literary form. He declares, therefore, or rather he confesses, proudly, that the "*Last Day of a Condemned Man*" is nothing less than a special pleading in favor of the abolition of the death penalty.

What he intended to do—what he wished that posterity might see in his work, if ever he goes down to it—is not the special defence, always easy to get together and always transitory, of any particular criminal—of any chosen offender. It is a general and permanent pleading for all accused, present or to come. It is the great point of the right of humanity, urged with the voice of earnestness before society, which is the great Court of Appeal! It is the supreme nonsuit—*abhorrescere a sanguine*—rising up forever in the face of every future criminal case. It is the sombre and fatal question which palpitates obscurely at the bottom of all capital causes, underneath the triple layers of pathos with which the bloody rhetoric of the prosecution envelops it. It is the question of life and death, I repeat, stripped naked, despoiled of the sonorous surroundings of the court of justice, brutally exposed to the light of day, and set up in a place where it must be seen, and where it must be kept—where it is really in its true place, in its horrible position: not in the tribunal, but on the scaffold—not in the hands of the judge, but in those of the executioner.

This is what the author wished to accomplish. If the future should award to him the glory of having done this, which he dares not to hope, he would wish for no other crown.

He proclaims, therefore, and he repeats it, he takes up this cause in the name of all possible accused, innocent or guilty,—before all courts, all tribunals, all juries, every sort of justice. This book is addressed to whomever may be capable of judging it. That the plea may be as vast as the cause—and it is for this reason that the "*Last Day of a Condemned Man*" is thus written—he has been obliged to divest his subject, in all its bearings, of the contingent, the accidental, the particular, the special, the relative, the modifiable, the episode, the anecdote, the event, the proper name; and to confine himself (if it may be so designated) to pleading the cause of an imaginary criminal, executed at an imaginary period, for an imaginary crime. Most happy, if, without any other implement than his own thoughts, he has penetrated deep enough to draw blood from a heart beating under the *æs triplex* of the magistrate! Most happy, if he has made pitiful those who believe themselves just! Most happy, if by dint of persecuting the judge he may succeed occasionally in finding in him the man!

Three years since, when this book appeared, some persons thought it worthwhile to dispute the originality of the author's idea. Some supposed it an English, others an American book. Strange mania of seeking the origin of things a thousand leagues off, and to ascribe to the Nile the water which washes your streets. Alas! this is neither an English nor an American book,—it is not even Chinese. The author took his idea of the "*Last Day of a Condemned Man*" not from a book,—he is not accustomed to going so far in search of his ideas,—but where you might all find it—where, perhaps, you have already found it (for who has not dreamed in his own mind the "*Last Day of a Condemned Man*"?)—simply on the public place—upon the Place de la Grève. [17] It was while passing there one day that he picked up this fatal idea, as it lay in a pool of blood, under the red pillars of the guillotine.

[17] The place of public execution at this epoch (1832).

Since then, each time that among the funereal Thursdays of the Court of Appeals there came one of those days when the cry of a death-sentence was heard in Paris—each time that the author heard under his windows the hoarse howlers who excite the spectators at the Grève—each time the saddening idea would return, would take possession of him, filling his head with armed men, with executioners, and with the crowd, and would expose to him, hour by hour, the last sufferings of the dying wretch. At this moment the priest confesses him—now they are cutting off his hair—now they are tying his hands. All this appealed to him—the poor poet—to tell what he felt to society, which goes about its daily business while this monstrous thing is being accomplished—hurried him, pushed him, shook him, tore his verses from his spirit if he was in the act of writing them and killed them at the instant that they were coming into life, stopped all his labors, crossed his path, in every way invested him, beset him, besieged him. It was a torment,—a torment that began with the day, and lasted, like that of the poor wretch who was being tortured at the same moment, until *four o'clock*. Then only, when the *ponens caput expiravit* was announced by the sinister voice of the great clock, the author breathed again, and found some freedom of spirit.

One day, at last,—it was, as well as he can remember, the day after the execution of Ulbach,—he set about writing this book. Since then he has been relieved. When one of those public crimes called judiciary executions has been committed, his conscience tells him that he is no longer responsible for it; and he has not since felt on his brow the drop of blood which, spouting up from the Grève, falls upon the head of every member of the social community. This, however, does not suffice. To wash one's hands of blood is well—to prevent its flowing would be still better.

He knows no more elevated aim, none more holy, none more august, than to aid in bringing about the abolition of the death penalty. And, from the bottom of his heart, he gives his adherence to the desires and the efforts of generous men of all nations who have worked for the past several years to cut down the fatal tree,—the only tree which revolutions have not been able to root up. It is with joy that he comes, feeble though he be, to give his stroke, and to enlarge with all his force the breach commenced by Beccaria sixty-six years ago in the old gibbet sanctioned for so many centuries by Christianity.

We have just said that the scaffold is the only edifice which revolutions do not demolish. It is rare, in fact, that revolutions are sparing of human blood; and, coming as they do to prune, to clear out, to lop off society, the death penalty is one of the chopping-knives which they relinquish with the greatest reluctance. We confess that if ever revolution seemed worthy and capable of abolishing the death penalty, it is the revolution of July. It seems, in fact, that it belonged to the most clement popular movement of modern times to scratch out the barbarous penal code of Louis XI., of Richelieu, and of Robespierre, and to inscribe in the face of the law the inviolability of human life. 1830 deserved to break the chopping-knife of '93.

We hoped it, for a moment. In August, 1830, there was so much generosity in the air, such a spirit of mildness and moderation floated in the masses, the heart felt itself so cheered by the approach of a glorious future, that it appeared to us that the death penalty had been abolished by common consent—by tacit and unanimous agreement—with the rest of the evil things which troubled us. The people had just made a bonfire of the rags of the ancient regime. This was the bloody rag,—we thought it was in the heap with the rest. We thought it was burnt up with others; and, for several weeks, confident and credulous, we had faith for the future in the inviolability of life as in the inviolability of liberty.

In fact, two months had hardly passed by before an attempt was made to reduce to a reality the sublime Utopia of Cæsar Bonesana.

Unhappily, this attempt was awkward, maladroit, almost hypocritical, and made in other than the general interest.

In the month of October, 1830, it may be remembered, several days after having dismissed by laying on the table the proposition to bury Napoleon under the column, the Chamber in a mass set to weeping and wailing. The question of the death penalty was brought up once again—we will say a few words further on, on this topic—and then it seemed that all the bowels of the legislators were taken with a sudden and marvellous compassion. It was who could speak, who could sigh, who could raise his hands higher to heaven! The death penalty, great God, what a horror!

A certain old *Procureur General* (State Attorney), grown white in his red gown, who all his life had eaten bread dipped in the blood of his petitioners, took all of a sudden a piteous mien, and called the gods to witness that he was outraged by the existence of the guillotine! During two days the tribune was filled with haranguers and mourners. It was a lamentation, a myriologue, a concert of lugubrious psalms, a *Super flumina Babylonis*, a *Stabat mater dolorosa*, a great symphony in *Do*, with choruses executed by the orchestra of orators who garnished the foremost benches of the Chamber, and who gave out such fine sounds in the great days. One came with his bass, another with his falsetto—nothing was lacking. The thing was to the last degree pathetic and pitiful. The night session was, above all, as tender, paternal, and heart-rending as the fifth act of one of Lachaussée's dramas. The good public, who understood nothing, stood with tears in its eyes!

What was the affair in question?—the abolition of the death penalty? Yes—and no.

Here are the facts. Four men of the upper circles, four men of elegant society—of the sort that one meets in drawing-rooms and with whom one might exchange occasionally a few polite words—four of these men, I say, had made in the high regions of politics one of those hardy attempts which Bacon calls *Crimes*, and Machiavel *Enterprises*. But crime or enterprise, the law, brutal for all, punishes it with death. And these four men were there, prisoners, captives by the law, guarded by three hundred tri-colored cockades, under the splendid ogives of Vincennes. What to do, and how to act? You understand that it is impossible to send to the Grève in a cart, ignobly tied with heavy ropes, back to back, with the functionary whom we dare not even name, four men like you and myself, four men of *good standing!* If there were but a guillotine in mahogany! Eh! we have nothing to do but to abolish the death penalty. [18]

[18] We do not pretend to envelop in the same disdain all that was said on that occasion in the Chamber. Here and there, noble and worthy words were uttered. We applauded, with everyone, the grave and simple discourse of Monsieur de Lafayette; and, of another color, the remarkable improvisation of Monsieur Villemain.

Thereupon, the Chamber set to work. Take notice, gentlemen, that yesterday only you treated this abolition as Utopian, theoretic, a dream, a madness, a poetic ideal. Take notice, gentlemen, that this is not the first time that your attention has been directed to the cart, to the hard ropes, and to the horrible scarlet machine,—and that it is strange that this hideous implement only now rises before your vision!

Bah! it is by this only that we are moved. It is not because of you, people, that we abolish the death penalty, but because of us deputies, who may one day be ministers. We will not have Guillotin's machine bite the higher classes. We will break it. If it suits anybody, so much the better; but we were only thinking of ourselves. Ucalegon is burning. Let us put out the fire. Quick, suppress the executioner!—strike at the code!

And it is thus that an alloy of egotism changes and prevents the finest social combinations. It is the black vein in white marble; it circulates throughout the mass, and appears at every moment unexpectedly under the chisel. Tour statue is to be carved over again.

Certainly it is not necessary to declare here that we are not among those who demand the heads of four ministers. As soon as these unfortunate men were arrested, the violent indignation which their attempt inspired was changed in us, as in everyone else, to a profound pity. We thought of the prejudices of education of some of them,—of the imperfectly developed brain of their chief, fanatical and obstinate remnant of the conspiracies of 1804, turned gray before his time in the damp shadows of state prisons,—of the fatal necessities of their common position,—of the impossibility of checking up on the rapid slope upon which the monarchy dashed itself unbridled the 8th of August, 1829,—of the too little-considered influence of the royal personage,—above all, of the dignity which one of them spread like a purple mantle over their misfortunes. We were of the number of those who wished most sincerely that their lives might be saved, and who were ready to devote ourselves to this end. If ever, by an impossibility, the scaffold had been set up on the Place de la Grève, we do not doubt that there would have been a riot to overturn it, and he who writes these lines would have been of that holy riot. For, it must be said, also, in social crises,—of all the scaffolds, the political scaffold is the most abominable, the most venomous, the most necessary to extirpate. This sort of guillotine takes root in the street pavement, and, in a little while, sprouts up on all parts of the soil.

In time of revolution, take care of the first head that falls. It awakens the popular appetite.

We were, therefore, personally, of the same opinion as those who wished to spare the four ministers,—of the same opinion, in every respect, for sentimental reasons and for political reasons. Only we would have liked better for the Chamber to have chosen another occasion to propose the abolition of the death penalty.

If this much to be desired abolition had been proposed, not in the case of four ministers fallen from the Tuileries into the prison at Vincennes, but in that of the first highway robber,—in that of one of the wretches whom you scarcely see when you pass him in the street, to whom you never speak, of whom you avoid instinctively the dusty contact,—an unhappy creature whose ragged childhood has run barefoot in the mud of the public places, shivering in winter on the edge of the Quais, warming itself at the window-gratings of the kitchens of M. Vefour, where you dine,—uncovering here and there a crust of bread in a heap of refuse and wiping it before devouring it, scratching all day in the gutter with a nail to find a farthing,—having no other amusement than the gratis spectacle of the king's fetes, and of the executions of La Grève, another gratis spectacle,—poor devils, driven by hunger to stealing, and from stealing to the rest of it,—children, disinherited by a stepmother society, that are adopted at twelve years by the house of correction, at eighteen by the galleys, and by the scaffold at forty,—unfortunate beings, whom, with a school or a workshop, you would have rendered good, moral, useful, and whom you do not know how to treat, casting them off as a useless burden, now into the red-ant hill of Toulon, and again into the mute enclosures of Clamart, cutting off their lives after having deprived them of their liberty! If it had been in the case of one of these men that you had proposed to abolish the death penalty, oh! then your session would have been really worthy, grand, holy, majestic, venerable. Since the august fathers of Trent, inviting heretics to the council in the name of God's entrails, *per viscera Dei*, because they hoped for their conversion, *quoniam sancta synadus sperat hæreticorum conversionem*, never assembly of men would have presented to the world a more sublime, a more illustrious, a more merciful spectacle. It has always been the part of those who are truly strong and truly great to have a care of the weak and the little.

A council of Brahmins would be great in taking in hand the cause of the pariah. And here the cause of the pariah was the cause of the people. In abolishing the death penalty for the people, and without waiting to have a personal interest in the question, you would have accomplished more than a political work, you would have accomplished a social one; whilst you have not even brought about a political object in trying to abolish it,—not to abolish it *per se*, but to save four unfortunate ministers, taken with their hands in the bag of the coup *d'état*.

What has happened? This,—as you were not sincere, you were not trusted. When the people saw that you wished to deceive them, they rose up *en masse* against the question, and, remarkable to state, they took part in favor of the death penalty, of which they support all the weight. It is your awkwardness which led to this. In dealing disingenuously with the question you compromised it for a long time. You were playing a comedy,—you were hissed.

This farce, nevertheless, some serious thinkers had the goodness to take in earnest. Immediately after the famous session, order was given to the prosecuting attorneys by an honest man, keeper of the seals, to suspend indefinitely all capital executions. This was in appearance a great step. The adversaries of the death penalty breathed again. But their illusion was of short duration.

The trial of the ministers was brought to a close. I do not know what sentence was passed. The four lives were spared. The fortress of Ham was chosen as a middle station between death and liberty. These divers arrangements once made, all fear vanished from the minds of the leading statesmen, and, with the fear, humanity disappeared. There was no longer any idea of abolishing capital punishment, and, as soon as there was no need of discussing it, Utopia became again Utopia; theory, theory; poesy, poesy.

There were, however, still in the prisons a few unhappy condemned, of the vulgar sort, who had been walking in the prison yards, taking the air, tranquilly, for five or six months, sure of living,—having taken their reprieve for their pardon. But, wait.

The executioner, in fact, had had a great fright. The day he had heard our law-makers talk humanity, philanthropy, progress, he thought himself lost. He hid himself, the wretch,—he had crept under his guillotine, as uncomfortable, under the sun of July as a night-bird in the full light of day, trying to be forgotten, closing his ears and hardly daring to take breath. He was not seen during six months. He gave no sign of life.

Little by little he reassured himself in his obscurity. He listened to the Chamber, and heard his name no longer mentioned. No more of those fine, sonorous words, that had frightened him so much. No more declamatory commentaries on the *Treatment of crime, and Punishments*. Other things occupied the Chamber—some grave social interest, a crossroad, a subvention for the Comic Opera, a bloodletting of a hundred thousand francs upon an apoplectic bill of fifteen hundred millions. No one thought of him, the headsman. Seeing which, he grew tranquil, put his head out of his hole, and looked around him. He made one step, then two, like the mouse in La Fontaine; then he ventures to come out entirely from under his scaffolding; then he mounts upon it, mends it, restores it, furbishes it, caresses it, makes it move, makes it shine, and then follows the action of the old rusted machine. Suddenly he turns, seizes in the nearest prison one of the unfortunate beings who counted on living, drags him to him, despoils him, fastens him, buckles him, and here the executions begin again.

All this is frightful, but it is history.

Yes, there was a reprieve of six months granted to these unhappy captives, whose situation was gratuitously aggravated by allowing them to hope for life, and then, without reason, without necessity, without knowing exactly why—*for the pleasure of the thing*, one fine morning, the reprieve was revoked, and all these human creatures were cut off in order. God! I ask what was it to us that these men might live? Is there not enough air in France for every man to get breath?

One day, a miserable clerk in a chancery court, to whom all this was perfectly indifferent, rose from his chair, saying, "Come; the abolition of the death penalty is no longer dreamed of; it is time to put up the guillotine again." In order that this should have occurred, something monstrous must have transpired in the heart of that man.

As a consequence, we may say that never were executions accompanied by more atrocious circumstances than since the revocation of the reprieve of July. Never has the history of the Grève been more revolting,—never has it better proven the execration of the death penalty. This increase of horror is the just chastisement of men who have restored to vigor the bloody code. May they be punished for their work! It is only right!

We must cite here two or three instances of the frightful and impious character of certain executions. We would like to torment the nerves of the wives of the king's prosecuting attorneys. A woman is sometimes a conscience.

In the south of France, towards the close of the month of September—we cannot exactly recall to mind the place, the day, or the name of the criminal, but we will find them if the fact should be contested,—and we are under the impression that it took place at Pamiers! Towards the end of last September, then, a man is sought put in his prison, where he was quietly playing at cards. It is signified to him, without warning, that he must die in two hours. He is seized with trembling in every limb, for, during six months, he was forgotten, and he did not count on dying. His hair is cut off, his beard shaven. He is bound, he is confessed, and then hustled off between four guards, through the crowd, to the place of execution. Up to this time, nothing but what is simple. It is thus that these things are done. Having reached the scaffold, the executioner takes him from the priest, carries him off, ties him down to the block, then let's go the knife. The heavy triangle of iron is detached with difficulty, falls joltingly in its grooves, and—here commences the horrible—chops the man, without killing him! The man utters a frightful cry. The executioner, disconcerted, lifts up the hatchet and lets it fall once more! The hatchet cuts into the patient's neck a second time, but does not cut through. The patient howls, and the crowd also. The executioner again hoists the hatchet, hoping better things of the third blow. Nothing of the sort. The third blow forces out a third stream of blood from the wretch's throat, but does not cause his head to fall. Let us cut short our story. The knife rises and falls five times! Five times it wounds the criminal, five times the criminal howls under the blow, and shakes his still living head, crying for mercy! The people, indignant, gathered stones, and commenced, in its justice, to stone the executioner. The executioner hid himself under the guillotine and behind the horses of the guards. But you are not yet at the end. The tortured man, seeing himself alone on the scaffold, lifted himself up from the block, and there standing, frightful, streaming with blood, sustaining his head, half cut off, which hung on his shoulder, he asked with feeble cries that someone would come to untie him. The crowd, full of pity, was on the point of forcing its way through the guards and coming to the assistance of the unhappy wretch who had thus endured five times his death sentence. At this moment the executioner's aid, a young man of twenty years, mounts upon the scaffold, tells the patient to turn that he may untie him, and, profiting by the posture of the dying man, who gave himself up without mistrust, jumped upon his back and set to cutting painfully what remained of the neck, with a sort of butcher's knife! This was done. This was seen. Yes!

According to the terms of the law, a judge should have assisted at this execution. By a sign, he could have stopped it all. What was he doing, buried in his carriage while this man was being massacred? What was he doing, this punisher of assassins, while, in broad daylight, under his eyes, under the breath of his horse's nostrils, under the glass of his coach door, a man was being assassinated?

And the judge was not called to judgment, and the executioner was not called to judgment! And no tribunal held inquest on this monstrous extermination of all laws in the sacred person of a creature of God!

In the seventeenth century, at the epoch of barbarism in the criminal code under Richelieu, under Christopher Fouquet, when M. de Chalais was put to death before le Bouffay de Nantes by an awkward soldier, who, instead of giving him one sword-thrust, gave him thirty-four blows with a cooper's truss, [19]—at least this appeared irregular to the Parliament of Paris. There was an inquest and a suit, and if Richelieu was not punished, if Fouquet was not punished, the soldier was. Injustice, without doubt; but at the bottom of which there was justice.

[19] La Porte says twenty-two, but Aubery says thirty-four. M. de Chalais cried out up to the twentieth.

Here, nothing. The affair took place after July, in a time of mild customs and of progress, one year after the celebrated lamentation of the Chamber on the death punishment, and yet the fact passed absolutely unperceived. The journals of Paris published it as an anecdote. No one is uneasy. It was only known that the guillotine had been disarranged on purpose by someone who wished to annoy the executioner. It was an aid of the executioner whom he had dismissed, who, to avenge himself, had played him this trick. It was only a childish amusement. Let us continue.

At Dijon, three months ago, a woman (a woman!) was led to the scaffold. This time, also, Dr. Guillotin's knife did its duty ill. The head was not quite cut off. Then the aids of the executioner harnessed themselves to the feet of the woman; and, while the woman sent up piercing yells, by dragging and jerking they finally tore the head from the body!

In Paris we are coming back to the practice of secret executions, as we do not dare decapitate on the public place of La Grève, as we are afraid, we are cowardly. This is what we do: lately, at Bicêtre, a man condemned to death, Desandrieux by name, I believe, was taken from his cell, put into a sort of basket on two wheels, closely shut up, padlocked and bolted; then, an armed guard before, an armed guard behind, noiselessly and without followers, this package was dragged off and deposited at the deserted barrier St. Jacques. Having reached this spot at eight o'clock in the morning, hardly daylight, there was found a guillotine just put up; for public, a few dozen little boys grouped on the heaps of stones which surrounded the unexpected machine. Quick! the man is drawn out from the basket, and, without giving him time to breathe, furtively, sullenly, shamefully, his head was juggled off. And this is called a public and solemn act of high justice! Infamous derision!

How do these people of the courts understand the word "civilization"? At what point are we? Justice vilified, in being reduced to stratagems and frauds! The law to expedients! Monstrous! A man condemned to death is a thing so formidable that society takes him treacherously in this fashion!

Let us be just, however; the execution was not altogether secret. In the morning the death-sentence was hawked about and sold in all the public places of Paris. It appears that there are persons who live by this sort of sale. Do you hear? Of the crime of an unfortunate creature, of his chastisement, of his tortures, of his agony, is made an article of commerce, a paper that is sold at one cent! Can you conceive anything more horrible than this cent turned to verdigris in blood? Who is it that can pick it up?

Here are facts enough—too many of them. Is not all this horrible? What have you to allege in favor of the death penalty? We ask this question seriously. We ask it, that it may be answered. We ask it of the criminal judges, not of mere writers of theories. We know that there are persons who take the excellence of the death penalty for a paradoxical text as they would take any other theme. There are others who like the death penalty only because they hate such or such a one who attacks it. It is for them a question quasi literary, a question of persons, a question of proper names. These are merely the envious, who are no more lacking to good jurisconsults than to great artists. The Joseph Greppas are no more lacking to the Filangieri than the Torregiani to Michael Angelo or the Scudery to Corneille.

It is not this class of men to whom we appeal, but to the men of the law, properly speaking, to the dialecticians, to the reasoners, to those who love the death penalty for its beauty, for its goodness, for its grace. Let them come on; let us hear their reasons.

Those who judge and condemn say that the death penalty is necessary; firstly, because it is of importance to amputate from the social community a member that has already injured it, and may injure it still more. If that were all, perpetual imprisonment would suffice. What is the advantage of the death? You object that it is possible to escape from prison. Keep better guard. If you do not believe in the solidity of iron bars, how dare you have menageries?

Let us have no executioner where the jailor suffices.

But, you recommence, society must avenge itself,—must punish. Neither the one nor the other. Vengeance is in the individual—punishment belongs to God.

Society is between the two. Chastisement is above it—vengeance below it. Nothing either so great or so little becomes it. It ought not to punish that it may avenge itself,—it ought *to correct that it may ameliorate.* Transform in this manner the formula of criminalists,—we understand it and we adhere to it.

There remains the third and last reason,—the theory of example. We must make examples. We must frighten by the spectacle of the fate reserved for criminals those who might be tempted to imitate them. This is nearly textually the eternal phrase of which the discourses of the judges of the five hundred courts are but the variations, more or less high sounding. Very well! We deny, firstly, that there is any example. We deny that the spectacle of the scaffold produces the effect expected of it. Far from edifying the people, it demoralizes and ruins in it all sensibility, all virtue. Proofs abound, and would but encumber our argument if we chose to cite them. We will point out, however, one in a thousand, because it is the most recent. At the moment that we write, only ten days have passed. It took place the fifth of March,—the last day of the Carnival. At Saint Paul—a village—immediately after the execution of an incendiary named Louis Camus, a troupe of masquers came and danced around the still smoking guillotine. Make examples, if you will,—a day of revel laughs you to scorn. If, however, in spite of your experience, you hang on to your routine theory of example, go back, then, to the sixteenth century; be truly formidable; give us back a variety of tortures; give us back Farinacci; give us back sworn torturers; give us back the gibbet, the wheel, the bastinado, the cropping of the ears, the quartering, the ditch for burying alive, the kettle for boiling alive; give us back, in all the public places of Paris, another shop added to the rest, the hideous stall of the executioner, always supplied with human flesh; give us back Montfaucon, its sixteen pillars of stone, its seated brutes, its caves full of bones, its beams, its hooks, its chains, its spits full of skeletons, its chalky heights spotted with crows, its branch gallows, and the odor of corpses which the north-east wind spread in great gusts all over the Faubourg of the Temple; give us back, in its permanence and its power, this gigantic apparatus of the executioner of Paris. Here is example on a grand scale! Here is the death penalty well understood! Here is a system of tortures which has some proportion! Here is the horrible, which is also terrible!

Or, at least, do as they do in England. In England—land of commerce—they take a smuggler on the coast of Dover, they hang him *for an example,* and *for an example* they leave him hooked to the gibbet; but, as the changes in the temperature might deteriorate the corpse, they envelope it carefully in a tarred cloth in order that they may not have to renew it so often. Oh, land of economy, where hanged men are tarred!

This, nevertheless, has something logical in it. It is the most humane fashion of interpreting the theory of example.

But you, do you think seriously that you make an example when you miserably cut the throat of a poor man in the most deserted corner of the outer boulevards? On the Grève, in broad daylight, may be admitted,—but at eight o'clock in the morning! Who passes there? Who goes there? Who knows that you are killing a man there? Who knows that you are making an example there? An example for whom? For the trees of the Boulevard, probably.

Do you not see, therefore, that your public executions are conducted slyly? Do you not see that you hide yourselves?—that you are afraid and ashamed of your work?—that you stammer out ridiculously your *discite justitiam moniti?*—that at bottom you are shaken, disconcerted, disquieted, little certain of being in the right, brought over by the general doubt, cutting off heads through routine, and without knowing exactly what you are doing? Do you not feel, at the bottom of your heart, that you have at least lost the moral and social sentiment of the mission of blood of your predecessors, the old parliamentists, accomplished with so tranquil a conscience? At night, do you not turn over on your uneasy pillow oftener than they? Others before you have ordered capital executions; but they believed themselves in the right, in justice, in well-doing. Jouvenel des Ursins believed himself a judge. Elie de Thorrette believed himself a judge. Laubardemont, La Reynie, and Laffemas themselves believed themselves judges. You, in your inner man,—you are not sure that you are not assassins.

You leave the Grève for the barrier Saint Jacques, the crowd for a solitude, the day for the twilight. You no longer do firmly what you have to do. You hide yourselves, I tell you.

Every reason for the death penalty is therefore overthrown. Here are all the syllogisms of the tribunal reduced to naught. All these shavings of legal discourse swept away and reduced to ashes. The lightest touch of logic dissolves all these bad reasonings.

Let the king's prosecutors come no more to demand heads of us jurors, of us men, adjuring us in soothing voice, in the name of a society to protect, of a public safety to secure, to make examples.

Rhetoric, inflation, and nothingness, all this! Stick a pin in all these hyperboles, and the air is all let out. At the bottom of this soft wordiness you find but hardness of heart, cruelty, barbarism, desire of proving one's zeal, necessity to gain better pay. Hold your tongues, mandarins? Under the velvet paw of the judge we feel the claws of the executioner.

It is difficult to think coolly on the nature of a royal criminal prosecutor. He is a man who earns his living by sending other men to the scaffold. He is the titled purveyor to the guillotine. Outside of this, he is a gentleman who has pretensions to style and to letters; who is a fine speaker, or thinks himself so; who recites, on occasion, a Latin verse or two before concluding the death sentence; who seeks to produce an effect, who looks to his own personal interest! oh, misery! when there are others whose lives are in question; who has his models, his types difficult to attain, his classics, his Bellart, his Marchangy, just as certain poets aim at Racine and certain others at Boileau. In the debate, he leans to the guillotine; it is in his part; it is his trade. His charge to the jury is his literary production. He embellishes it with flowers of metaphor; he perfumes it with quotations; he must make it elegant, for his audience; it must please the ladies. He has his baggage of commonplaces, even yet very new for the provinces,—his charms of elocution, his researches, his refinements of the writer. He hates the proper noun almost as much as our tragic poets of Delille's school. Never fear that he will call things by their right names. For shame! He has, for any idea the nakedness of which might revolt you, whole suits of disguises in epithets and adjectives. He renders Monsieur Samson (the executioner) presentable. He veils the hatchet. He colors the block. He wraps up the red basket in a periphrase. No one can see what it is. It is genteel and decent.

Can you figure to yourself this man, at night in his closet, elaborating at his leisure and to the best of his powers, this harangue which will set up the guillotine in six weeks? Do you see him sweating blood and water in order to shut up the head of an accused in the most fatal article of the code? Do you see him sawing with an ill-made law the neck of a miserable creature? Do you remark how he infuses two or three venomous texts in a slop of tropes and synecdoches, to express out of it and extract from it with great pains the death of a man? Is it not true that, while he writes, under his table, in the shadow, he has the executioner crouching at his feet, and that he stops now and then, as he dips his pen in his inkstand, to say to him, like a master to his dog, "Be quiet, be quiet,—you shall have your bone "?

And yet, in private life, this man of the law may be an honest man, good father, good son, good husband, good friend,—as all the epitaphs in Père Lachaise tell us.

Let us hope that the day is at hand when the law will abolish all these funereal functions. The very air of our civilization ought, in a given time, to wear out the death penalty.

We are sometimes tempted to believe that the defenders of the death penalty have not reflected what it is. But weigh a little in the balance of the most outrageous crime this exorbitant right which society arrogates to itself of taking away what it has not given— this punishment the most irreparable of irreparable punishments.

Either one thing or the other. Either the man whom you strike down is without family, without parents, without adherents, in this world,—and, in this case, he has received neither education, nor instruction, nor care of his mind, nor of his heart; and then, what right have you to kill this wretched orphan? You punish him, because, since his childhood, he has grovelled on the soil, without support and without a tutor. You impute to him as a crime the isolation in which you have left him. Of his misfortune you make his criminality. No one ever taught him to know what he was doing. This man is ignorant—his fault is his destiny. You strike an innocent man.

Or, this man has a family; and then, do you believe that the wound which puts an end to him reaches him only,—that his father, his mother, his children, do not bleed, too? No, in killing him, you decapitate a whole family. And here, also, you strike the innocent.

Clumsy and blind penalty, which, no matter to which side it turns, strikes the innocent.

This man, this guilty creature, who has a family, lock him up. In his prison he can still work for his children. But how will he earn their living in his tomb? And, can you think without a shiver of what will become of these little girls—of these little boys— whose father you take from them, and with him, their bread? Is it that you count on this family to supply the galleys and the houses of prostitution fifteen years later? Ah! the poor, innocent creatures!

In the colonies, when a death sentence kills a slave there are a thousand francs indemnity awarded to the proprietor of the man. What, you make amends to the master, and you do not indemnify the family? In this latter case, do you not take a man away from those who possess him? Is he not, by a much more sacred title than the slave to his master, the property of his father, the goods of his wife, the thing of his children?

We have already convicted your law of assassination. Here we convict it of theft.

Yet another thing. The soul of this man—do you think of it? Do you know in what state it may be? Do you dare to expedite it so lightly? In former times, at least, some faith circulated among the people; at the last agony, the religious breath which was in the air might soften the most hardened; a patient was at the same time a penitent; religion opened a new world to him at the moment that society closed this old one; every soul had knowledge of God; the scaffold was only a frontier of heaven. But what hope do you put upon the scaffold, now that the great crowd no longer believes,—now that all religions are attacked by the dry rot, like the old vessels that are mouldering away in our ports,— now that little children mock at God? By what right do you launch these obscure souls of your condemned into a something of which you have doubts yourself? These souls, such as Voltaire and M. Pigault Lebrun has made them,—you hand them over to the chaplain of the prison, an excellent old man, without doubt,—but does he believe himself, and does he inspire belief? Does he not go through with his sublime work as if it were a task? Do you take this good man for a priest,—he who elbows the executioner in the cart? A writer, full of soul and talent, has said before us, "*It is a horrible thing to keep the executioner, after having taken away the confessor!*"

These are, without doubt, mere sentimental reasons, as the disdainful, who only find their logic in their heads, would say. In our eyes they are the best. We often prefer reasons of sentiment to reasons of reason.

Besides, we must not forget the two series are always closely connected. The "*Traité des Délits*" is grafted on *L'Esprit des Lois*. Montesquieu engendered Beccaria.

Reason is with us, sentiment is with us, experience also is with us. In model states, where the death penalty is abolished, the mass of capital crimes follow from year to year a progressive decrease. Weigh this.

We do not ask, for the present, a hasty and complete abolition of the death penalty, like the one so giddily entered into by the Chamber of Deputies. We desire, on the contrary, all the trials—all the gropings—of prudence. Besides, we do not merely wish the abolition of the death penalty; we wish for a complete revision of penalty in all its forms from top to bottom, from the bolt to the hatchet, and time is one of the ingredients which must enter into a work of this kind, in order that it may be well done. We intend to develop elsewhere, upon this matter, the system of ideas which we believe applicable. But, independently of partial abolitions in the case of false money, of incendiary attempts, of thefts, etc., we demand that from this time in all capital affairs the president shall be required to put this question to the jury, "*Has the accused acted, through passion or interest?*" And that, in case the jury shall reply, "the accused has acted through passion," there shall be no condemnation to death. This will at least spare us a few revolting executions. Ulbach and Debacker would have been saved. Othellos would be no more guillotined.

In fact, that no one be deceived, this question of the death penalty is ripening every day. Before long, the whole of society will resolve it as we do.

Let the most obstinate criminalists take heed. For a century, the death punishment has been on the decline. It has become almost mild,—sign of decrepitude, sign of weakness, sign of approaching death. The torture has disappeared; the wheel has disappeared; the gallows has disappeared. Strange fact,—the guillotine is a progress.

Monsieur Guillotin was a philanthropist.

Yes, the horrible Themis, sharp-toothed and voracious, of Farinace and of de Vouglans, of Delancre and of Isaac Loisel, of d'Oppede and de Machault, is wasting away. She grows weaker,—she is dying.

Already the Grève will not receive her. The Grève is reinstated in her rights. The old blood drinkers behaved well in July. She wishes hereafter to lead a better life, and to remain worthy of her last noble act. She who for three centuries prostituted herself to all scaffolds, is seized with a sense of shame. She is ashamed of her former trade. She wishes to lose her ugly name. She repudiates the executioner. She washes her pavement.

At this moment the death penalty is already out of Paris; and, we may say it, to go out of Paris is to go out from civilization.

All the symptoms are in our favor. It appears to us, too, that she is disgusted, she is sullen,—this hideous machine, or, rather, this monster made of wood and iron, which is to Guillotin what Galatea was to Pygmalion. Seen from a certain point of view, the frightful executions of which we gave the details on a former page are excellent signs.

The guillotine hesitates; she has failed in her stroke. The entire old scaffolding of the death penalty is tumbling to pieces.

The infamous machine will leave France. We count on it; and, if it pleases God, she will march off lamely, for we will try to fetch her some rude blows.

Let her go ask hospitality elsewhere,—of some barbarous nation. Not of Turkey, where civilization is dawning,—not of the savages, [20] who would not have her,—but let her descend a few rounds of the ladder of civilization. Let her go to Spain or to Russia.

[20] The parliament of Otaheite has just abolished the death penalty.

The social edifice of the past reposed upon three columns,—the *priest, the king, and the executioner*. It is already a long time since a voice said, "*the gods are departing.*" Lately, another voice was raised, crying, "*The kings are departing.*" It is time now that another Voice should arise, and say, "*The executioner is departing.*"

Thus, ancient society will have fallen, stone by stone; and Providence will have completed the crumbling of the past.

To those who regretted the gods, it has been proclaimed, "God remains." To those who regret kings, it may be said, "the country remains." To those who would regret the executioner, nothing remains to be said.

And public order will not disappear with the executioner. Do not believe it. The arch of the future social fabric will not fall in for the lack of this hideous key-stone. Civilization is nothing more than a series of successive transformations. To what, then, will you lend your presence? To the transformation of the penal code? The mild law of Christ will penetrate the code at last, and will shine through it. Crime will be regarded as a disease, and this disease will have its physicians, who will replace your judges. Its hospitals will replace, your galleys. Liberty and health will resemble each other. Where iron and fire were applied, we will pour on balm and oil. The evil that was treated by anger we will treat with charity. It will be simple and sublime. The cross substituted for the gibbet. Only this.

March 15, 1832.

A COMEDY,

SUGGESTED BY A TRAGEDY. [21]

[21] We have thought fit to reprint this sort of preface in dialogue which follows, and which accompanied the fourth edition of the "*Last Day of a Condemned Man.*" It must be recollected, while reading it, in the midst of what political objections, as well as moral and literary, the first editions of this book were published.

PERSONAGES.

MADAME DE BLINVAL,	A PHILOSOPHER,
LE CHEVALIER,	A STOUT GENTLEMAN,
ERGASTE,	A THIN GENTLEMAN,
UN POETE ELEGIAQUE,	LADIES,
A LACKEY.	

Scene.—A Drawing-Room.

THE ELEGIAC POET (*reading*).

"The morrow, footsteps traversed the forest
Along the river bank wandered a dog unrest.
And when the lady of the bark, in tears,
Returned and sat down, her heart filled with fears,
Upon the mouldering towers of the antique castle,
    She heard the waters sigh, the sad Isaurin;
    But heard no more the mandolin
        Of the gentle minstrel!"

THE WHOLE AUDIENCE.

Bravo! charming! magnificent! (*They clap their hands*).

MADAME BLINVAL.

There is in this closing scene an indefinable mystery which draws tears from the eyes.

THE ELEGIAC POET.

The catastrophe is veiled.

THE CHEVALIER (*throwing back his head.*)

Mandolin, minstrel, that is of the romantic school! [22]

[22] *Note by the translator.*—At the time this work first appeared the great war was waging between the classic and romantic schools, of which latter Victor Hugo was the chief.

THE ELEGIAC POET.

Yes, sir; but of the reasonable romantic school—of the true romantic school. What can we do? We are forced to make some concessions.

THE CHEVALIER.

Concessions! Concessions! that is the way all true taste is lost. I would give, all the verses of the romantic school for this single quatrain,—

"De par le Pinde et par Cythère,
Gentil Bernard est averti
Que l'Art d'Aimer doit samedi
Venir souper chez l'Art de Plaire."

This is true poetry! *The Art of Love who sups on Saturday with the Art of Pleasing!* At least we have something. But, today, it is *the mandolin, the minstrel*. No one thinks any more of making *fugitive poetry*; but I am no poet myself.

THE ELEGIAC POET.

Elegies, however.

THE CHEVALIER.

Fugitive poetry, sir. (*Low, to Mme. de Blinval.*) And then *castle* is not French; we say *castel*.

SOME ONE. (*to the elegiac poet*).

One observation, sir. You say the *antique* castle,—why not gothic?

THE ELEGIAC POET.

Gothic is not used in verse.

SOMEONE.

Ah, that makes a difference!

THE ELEGIAC POET (*continuing*).

Do you observe, sir, we must limit ourselves. I am not of the set who wish to disorganize French verse, and to take us back to the time of the Ronsard and the Brébeuf. I am a romantic, but a moderate one. I am just the same for emotions. I like them sweet, dreamy, melancholy—never blood, never horrors. Veiled catastrophes. I know there are persons, madmen with imaginations in delirium, who—By the way, ladies, have you read the new novel?

THE LADIES.

What novel?

THE ELEGIAC POET.

The Last Day—

A STOUT GENTLEMAN.

Enough, sir! I know what you intend to say. The title alone sets my nerves trembling.

MADAME DE BLINVAL.

And mine, too. It is a frightful book. I have it here.

THE LADIES.

Let us see! Let us see! (*The book is passed around.*)

SOMEONE (reading).

The Last Day of a—

THE STOUT GENTLEMAN.

I beg, madame!

MADAME DE BLINVAL.

In fact, it is an abominable book—a book which gives you the nightmare—a book that makes you sick.

A LADY (*speaking low*).

I must positively read it.

THE STOUT GENTLEMAN.

We must admit that public morals are becoming more and more depraved every day. Good God, the horrible idea! To develop, to search into, to analyze one after another, without leaving out a single one, all the physical sufferings, all the moral tortures, which a man condemned to death must experience the day of his execution. Is it not truly atrocious? Can you understand, ladies, that a writer could be found for this idea, and a public for tin's writer?

THE CHEVALIER.

It is really a sovereign impertinence.

MADAME. DE BLINVAL.

"What is this author?

THE STOUT GENTLEMAN.

There was no name to the first edition.

THE ELEGIAC POET.

He is the same who has already written two novels; but I have really forgotten their titles. The first commences at the Morgue and finishes at the Grève. In each chapter there is an ogre that devours a child.

THE STOUT GENTLEMAN.

Have you read that, sir?

THE ELEGIAC POET.

Yes, sir; the scene is laid in Iceland.

THE STOUT GENTLEMAN.

In Iceland! That is frightful.

THE ELEGIAC POET.

Besides this, he has written odes, ballads, a pack of other things, in which there are monsters with blue bodies (*corps bleus*).

THE CHEVALIER (*laughing*).

Corbleu! That must be a furious sort of verse.

THE ELEGIAC POET.

He has also published a drama—or, at least, he calls it a drama—in which there is this handsome line,—

"Tomorrow, the twenty-fifth of June, sixteen hundred and fifty-seven."

SOMEONE.

Ah, this fine line!

THE ELEGIAC POET.

It may be written in figures, you see, ladies,—Tomorrow, 25th June, 1657. (*He laughs. All the rest laugh.*)

THE CHEVALIER.

The poesy of the present day is of a very remarkable sort.

THE STOUT GENTLEMAN.

Bless me! he does not know how to versify, that man? What may be his name, pray?

THE ELEGIAC POET.

He has a name as difficult to recall as to pronounce. There is a little of the goth, [23] the visigoth, and the ostrogoth in it. (*He laughs.*)

[23] *Goth.* Pronounced *go.*

MADAME DE BLINVAL.

He is a bad man.

THE STOUT GENTLEMAN.

An abominable man.

A WOMAN.

A person who knows him tells me—

THE STOUT GENTLEMAN.

You know someone who knows him?

THE YOUNG WOMAN.

Yes; and who says that he is an amiable and excellent man, who lives in a retired way, and spends his days playing with his grandchildren.

THE POET.

And his nights in dreaming of works of darkness. See, this is strange. I have made a line of poetry, quite naturally, really. Here it is,—

And his nights in dreaming of works of darkness.

The requisite number of feet. There remains only to find a suitable rhyme. Pardieu!

MADAME DE BLINVAL.

Quidquid tentabit dicere, versus erat.

THE STOUT GENTLEMAN.

You said that the author in question has grandchildren. Impossible, madam. A man who has written such a tale! An atrocious tissue!

SOMEONE.

But what is the end he wished to attain in writing it?

THE ELEGIAC POET.

How should I know?

THE PHILOSOPHEB.

It appears that his end is to aid in bringing about the abolition of the death penalty.

THE STOUT GENTLEMAN.

A horror, I tell you!

THE CHEVALIER.

Indeed! It is a duel engaged with the executioner.

THE ELEGIAC POET.

He has a terrible spite against the guillotine.

THE THIN GENTLEMAN.

That is evident, at a glance! Mere declamation!

THE STOUT GENTLEMAN.

Not at all. There are hardly two pages on the topic of the death penalty. All the rest is filled up with sensations.

THE PHILOSOPHER.

Here is the mistake. The subject demands argument. A drama, a romance, proves nothing. And, besides, I have read the book, and it is bad.

THE ELEGIAC POET.

Detestable! Is that what may be called art? It goes beyond all bounds; it breaks loose from everything. Furthermore, this criminal—if I only knew who he might be! Nothing of the sort. What has he done? I am not even told this. He may, after all, be a very contemptible wretch. No one has a right to interest me in a person whom I do not know.

THE STOUT GENTLEMAN.

No one has a right to expose his readers to actual physical suffering. When I go to see a tragedy, where there are murders, I can bear them. But this novel—it makes your hair stand on end; it makes your blood run cold; it gives you bad dreams. I was ill in bed for two days after reading it.

THE PHILOSOPHER.

Add to this that it is a cold and calculating book.

THE POET.

A book! A book!

THE PHILOSOPHER.

Yes. And as you said just now, sir, it is not in it that we find the veritable aesthetics. I cannot take an interest in an abstraction,—in pure entity. I do not see in it a personality adequate to my own. And, then, the style is neither simple nor pure. It has the odor of archaism. This is what you were remarking just now, is it not?

THE POET.

Of course, of course. We want no personalities.

THE PHILOSOPHER.

The criminal is not at all interesting.

THE POET.

How can he be interesting? He has committed a crime and has no remorse. I would have done just the contrary. I would have related the history of my criminal. Born of honest parents; a good education; love; jealousy; a crime which was not a crime; and then remorse, remorse, continually remorse. But human laws are implacable; he must die. And, at this point, I should have treated my question of the death penalty. This would be the true way!

MADAME DE BLINVAL.

Ah! ah!

THE PHILOSOPHER.

Excuse me. The book, as Mr.—comprehends it, would prove nothing. Single cases do not establish a general rule.

THE POET.

Very well! Better still! Why not have chosen, for example, Malesherbes, the virtuous Malesherbes,—his last day, his execution? In that case,—grand and noble spectacle!—I would have wept; I would have shuddered; I would have wished to mount the scaffold with him.

THE PHILOSOPHER.

Not I.

THE CHEVALIER.

Nor I. In reality your Monsieur de Malesherbes was a revolutionary.

THE PHILOSOPHER.

The scaffold of Malesherbes proves nothing against the death penalty in general.

THE STOUT GENTLEMAN.

The death penalty! Why pay any attention to it? What is it to you, the death penalty? This author must be of very low birth that he thinks fit to give us the nightmare on this subject, with his book.

MADAME DE BLINVAL.

Yes, indeed; a bad-hearted man!

THE STOUT GENTLEMAN.

He forces us to look into prisons, into the galleys, into Bicêtre. It is extremely disagreeable. It is well known that these places are filthy sewers; but what is that to society?

MADAME DE BLINVAL.

Those who made the laws were not mere children.

THE PHILOSOPHER.

Ah! nevertheless, in presenting things with truth—

THE THIN GENTLEMAN.

But this is precisely what is lacking,—truth. How can you expect a poet to know anything of such matters? It is necessary to be, at the least, a prosecuting attorney. Listen! I read in a newspaper an extract from this book, where it was affirmed that when the death sentence was read to the condemned, he said not a word! Very well for my part, I saw a criminal once, who, when his sentence was read to him, gave a loud cry. So you see!

THE PHILOSOPHER.

Allow me—

THE THIN GENTLEMAN.

Remark, gentlemen, the guillotine, the Grève, are bad taste; and the proof of this is that it appears that this book corrupts the taste, and renders one incapable of fresh, pure, naive emotions. When will the defenders of a healthy literature come forth? I wish that I were—and, in fact, my criminal charges may give me a right to offer myself as a member of the French Academy. Let me appeal to Monsieur Ergastes, who is one of that learned body. What does he think of "*The Last Day of a Condemned Man*"?

ERGASTES.

In fact, sir, I have not read it; and I shall not read it. I dined yesterday with Madame de Sénange; and the Marchioness of Morival was speaking of the work to the Duke of Melcourt. I am told that there are personal allusions to the magistracy, and particularly to President d'Alimont. The abbé de Floricour was also indignant. It appears that there is also a chapter against religion, and a chapter against monarchy. If I were the king's attorney—

THE CHEVALIER.

King's attorney, forsooth! and the charter! and the liberty of the press! Nevertheless, a poet who wishes to suppress the death penalty, you must admit that it is odious—oh, oh! in the ancient régime just imagine anyone writing a book against the torture! But, since the taking of the Bastille, anything may be printed. Books do a frightful deal of harm.

THE STOUT GENTLEMAN.

Frightful, indeed! We were tranquil; we thought of nothing. Now and then in France a head here and there was cut off; at the most, two in a week. All that without noise or scandal. They said nothing,—no one thought of it,—not in the least; and here is a book—a book that gives you a terrible headache!

THE THIN GENTLEMAN.

No jury can condemn after having read it!

ERGASTES.

It troubles men's consciences.

MADAME DE BLINVAL.

Ah, books! books! Who would have believed this of a novel?

THE POET.

It is quite certain that books are frequently a poison subversive of social order.

THE THIN GENTLEMAN.

Without taking into consideration the language, which the romantics are revolutionizing at the same time.

THE POET.

There is a distinction, sir,—a great difference between writers of the romantic school.

THE THIN GENTLEMAN.

Bad taste,—bad taste!

ERGASTES.

You are right. Bad taste!

THE THIN GENTLEMAN.

There is no answering this.

THE PHILOSOPHER (*leaning over the arm of a lady's chair*).

They are saying things there that are not even allowed in the Rue Mouffetard (the rag-pickers' quarter).

ERGASTES.

Ah! the abominable book!

MADAME DE BLINVAL.

Oh, do not throw it in the fire! It belongs to the Circulating Library.

THE CHEVALIER.

Talk of our day! How everything is depraved since—taste and manners! Do you remember how it was in our day, Madame de Blinval.

MADAME DE BLIUVAL.

No, sir; it does not remember me.

THE CHEVALIER.

We were the gayest, the mildest, the most witty people,—always elegant festivities, pretty verses,—it was charming. Is there anything more gallant than the Madrigal which Monsieur de la Harpe wrote on the grand ball given by Madame the Marechale de Mailly in the year seventeen hundred—the year of the execution of Damiens?

THE STOUT GENTLEMAN (*sighing*).

Happy time! At present morals are horrible, and books as well. One of Boileau's fine lines says the downfall of morals follows that of the arts.

THE PHILOSOPHER (*low to the poet*).

Do they have supper in this house?

THE ELEGIAC POET.

Yes, presently.

THE THIN GENTLEMAN.

Now they wish to abolish the death penalty, and, to this end, they make cruel and immoral novels in bad taste. "*The Last Day of a Condemned Man*" and the like.

THE STOUT GENTLEMAN.

I beg, dear sir, that you will not speak of this atrocious book again; and, since we have the pleasure of meeting, tell me what are you to do with the man whose appeal was rejected about three weeks since?

THE THIN GENTLEMAN.

Ah, a little patience! I am on a holiday here, let me breathe a bit; on my return. If the delay is too great, however, I will write to my substitute—

A LACKEY (*entering*).

Madame, supper is served.

THE LAST DAY OF A CONDEMNED MAN.

I.

Condemned to death!

It is now five weeks that I dwell with this thought—alone with it—always frozen by its presence, always bowed down under its weight.

Once, for it appears to me that years have passed instead of weeks, I was a man like any other man. Each day, each hour, each minute had its idea. My mind, young and rich, was tilled with fancies. It amused itself in unrolling them to me one after another, without order and without end, embroidering with inexhaustible arabesques this same uneven and delicate fabric of life. There were young girls, splendid bishops stoles, battles fought and won, theatres full of noise and light, and again young girls, and twilight promenades under the shadowing branches of chestnut trees. There was always a gala in my imagination,—I could think as I chose. I was free.

Now I am captive. My body is in irons in a dungeon; my mind is imprisoned in an idea,—a horrible, a bloody, an implacable idea! I have only one thought, one conviction, one certainty! condemned to death!

Whatever I do this infernal thought, like a leaden spectre, is always present, alone and jealous, driving away all diversion; face to face with me, wretched, and shaking me with its two icy hands when I would turn aside my head or close my eyes. It glides under all the forms to which my spirit would escape,—mingles itself, like a horrible burden of a song, with every word which is addressed to me,—glues itself with me to the hideous gratings of my dungeon; besets me awake, spies me in my convulsive sleep, and reappears in my dreams under the form of a knife.

I have just awaked with a start, pursued by it, and saying to myself, "Ah, it is only a dream!" And even before my heavy eyes have had time to open wide enough to see this fatal thought written in the horrible reality which surrounds me, upon the damp and sweating pavement of my cell, in the pale rays of my night-lamp, and the coarse texture of my clothing,—on the sombre face of the soldier on guard, whose bayonet shines through the grating of the dungeon. It seems to me that already I hear a voice murmuring in my ear "*Condemned to Death!*"

II.

It was a fine morning in August. My suit had been three days in court. For three successive days my name and my crime had rallied a crowd of spectators, who came to alight upon the benches of the audience chamber like crows around a corpse. Three days that all this phantasmagoria of judges, of witnesses, of lawyers, of king's attorneys, passed and repassed before me, sometimes grotesque, sometimes bloody, always gloomy and fatal.

The first two nights I could not sleep from anxiety and terror; the third I had slept from fatigue and lassitude. At midnight I had left the jury deliberating,—I had been led off to the straw of my dungeon, and I had fallen instantaneously in a profound sleep,—sleep of oblivion! They were my first hours of repose for many days.

I was still in the heaviest moment of my slumbers when they came to awaken me. This time neither the heavy tread of the iron-soled shoes of the jailor, nor the rattling of his bunch of keys, nor the hoarse grating of the bolts, sufficed to arouse me from my lethargy. He was obliged to lay his Tough hand on my arm, and to cry in my ears, "Get up! get up!" to announce his presence. I opened my eyes, and sat up, bewildered. At this moment, through the narrow and lofty window of my cell, I saw on the ceiling of the neighboring corridor—the only sky granted me—that yellow tint in which the dwellers in the darkness of prison-walls learn so well to recognize as the sun. I love the sun!

"The weather is fine," said I to the jailor.

He remained a moment without replying to me, as if uncertain whether it was worthwhile to waste any words on me. Then, with an effort, he muttered roughly,—

"That may be."

I remained motionless, my spirit still half asleep, my lips smiling, my eye fixed upon that mild, golden reflection, which mottled the ceiling.

""We have a beautiful day," I repeated.

"Yes," replied the man, "they are waiting for you."

These few words, like the thread which checks the flight of an insect, brought me back violently to the reality. I saw again, as if in a lightning's flash, the sombre court-room, the judges' horse-shoe desk, loaded with bloody rags, the three rows of stupid faced witnesses, the two guards at the ends of my bench, the black robes rustling and agitated, the heads of the crowd, the back-ground, and turned on me the fixed looks of those twelve, jurymen who had watched while I slept.

I rose. My teeth chattered; my hands trembled, and could not reach my clothing; my limbs failed under me. The first steps that I made I staggered like a porter under a too heavy burden. Nevertheless, I followed the jailor.

The two guards awaited me at the door of my cell. They put on my handcuffs again. They had a little complicated lock which was shut with care. I made no resistance. Their handcuffs were a machine upon another machine.

We crossed an interior court. The sharp morning air revived me. I raised my head. The sky was blue; and the warm rays of the sun, intercepted by the tall chimneys, traced great angles of light on the cornices of the high and gloomy prison-walls. It was a lovely morning.

"We ascended a winding stairway. We passed through one corridor, then another, then a third, then a low door opened. A warm air, mingled with murmuring voices, struck me in the face. It was the breath of the crowd assembled in the courtroom. I went in.

On my appearance there was a sound of arms and of voices. The benches were pushed noisily about. The partition-boards cracked; and, as I crossed the long hall, between two masses of people walled in by soldiers, it seemed to me that I was the centre to which were attached the threads which put in motion all the staring and eager faces.

At this moment I perceived that my irons had been removed, but I could not recall where or when they had been taken off.

Then there came a deep silence. I had reached my place. The instant that the tumult in the crowd ceased, it ceased also in my ideas. I understood at once clearly what I had only confusedly perceived until then—that the decisive moment had come, that I was there to hear my sentence!

Explain it who can, from the manner in which this idea came to me, it caused me no terror. The windows were open! The air and noise of the city entered freely from without! The hall was as light as if for a wedding; the gay rays of the sun traced here and there luminous figures of the window frames—sometimes elongated upon the floor, sometimes spread out on the tables or by the angles of the walls, and from these dazzling window lozenges each beam cut out in relief a great prism of golden dust.

The judges at the farther end of the hall looked satisfied, probably at the happiness of soon bringing the case to a close. The visage of the presiding judge, mildly lit up by the reflection from a window-pane, had something calm and good in it; and a young judge's assistant, playing with his neckband, talked almost gaily with a lady in a pink bonnet, who, as a favor, was seated behind him.

The jurymen alone looked pale and worn; but it was apparently from the fatigue of sitting up all night. Some of them yawned. Nothing in their countenances announced men who had just pronounced a death sentence, and in the faces of these good citizens I could only discover a great desire to go to sleep.

Opposite to me was a wide open window. I heard the flower-women laughing on the quays; and on the edge of the window-sill a delicate little yellow plant, penetrated by a sunbeam, played with the wind in a crack of the stone.

How could a sinister idea dawn among so many graceful sensations? Bathed in air and sunshine, it was impossible for me to think of anything but liberty. Hope shone with me in harmony with the light around me; and confident, I awaited my sentence as one might await deliverance and life.

Meanwhile my lawyer arrived. They were waiting for him. He had just eaten a copious breakfast with a hearty appetite. When he reached his place, he leaned over towards me, with a smile, and said,—

"I have hopes."

"And I, too," replied I, light and smiling also.

"Yes," he resumed, "I know nothing as yet of their verdict; but they have doubtless set aside premeditation, and it will only be the galleys for life."

"What do you say, sir?" replied I; with indignation. "Better death, a hundred times!"

Yes, death! And, after all, what do I risk in saying this? Was a death sentence ever pronounced except by torch-light at midnight, in a dark, gloomy hall, and on a cold, rainy winter's night? In the month of August, at eight o'clock in the morning, on so bright a day, these good jurymen—it is impossible! And my eyes turned once more to the pretty little flower in the sunbeam.

Suddenly the presiding judge, who had only waited for my lawyer, requested me to stand up. The soldiers carried arms, and, as if by an electric movement, the whole assembly arose at the same instant. An insignificant individual, seated at a table lower down than the tribune,—he was the clerk, I believe,—began to speak, and read the verdict which the jury had pronounced in my absence. A cold sweat broke out all over me; I leaned against the wall to prevent myself from falling.

"Advocate, have you anything to say against the passing of the sentence?"

I, myself, had everything to say, but nothing suggested itself. My tongue was glued to the roof of my mouth.

The defending advocate rose. I understood that he sought to attenuate the verdict of the jury, and to place under it, instead of the penalty it suggested, the other penalty, the one which offended me so much when I saw that he hoped for it.

My indignation must have been very great to find vent in the tumult of emotions which distracted my thoughts. I wished to repeat aloud what I had already said to him, "Death a hundred times in preference." But my breath failed me, and I could only seize him rudely by the arm, crying out, with convulsive force, "No!"

The prosecuting attorney opposed the defense, and I listened with a stupid satisfaction. Then the judges went out, then returned, and the presiding judge read me my sentence.

"Condemned to death!" repeated the crowd, and, while they led me away, all these people precipitated themselves on my footsteps with the crash of an edifice falling in. I moved on, drunk and stupefied. A revolution had taken place within me. Until the death sentence was passed, I felt myself breathe, palpitate, live, in the same atmosphere as other men—now I distinguished a sort of wall built up between the world and myself. Nothing appeared under the same aspect as before. Those wide windows, this brilliant sunlight, this pure sky, that pretty flower, all had turned as pale and as white as a winding-sheet. These men, these women, these children, who hurried across my path,—I found in them a look of phantoms.

At the foot of the stairway a black and dirty grated carriage was waiting for me. As I got into it, I looked by chance upon the public place. "Condemned to death" cried out the passers-by, hurrying up to the carriage. Through the cloud which seemed interposed between the outer world and myself, I distinguished two young girls who followed me with eager eyes. "How nice," said the younger one. "It will take place in six weeks!"

III.

Condemned to death!

And why not? *Men*, I remember once to have read in a book in which this was the only good thing—*Men are all condemned to death, with an indefinite reprieve*. At least, what is there changed in my condition?

Since the hour in which my sentence was pronounced, how many are dead who counted on long life! How many have gone before me, who, young, free, and full of health, expected to go at such an hour, on such a day, to see my head fall, on the Place de la Grève! How many more are there now moving about and breathing the pure air, going out and coming in at their good pleasure, who will go before me!

And then, what is there in life so much to be regretted by me? In fact, the obscurity, the black bread of the dungeon, the portion of poor broth dipped out of the prisoner's bucket; to be spoken to roughly—I, refined by education, to be brutalized by gaolers and prison-guards, not to see a human being who considers me worthy of being spoken to and to whom I can reply, ceaselessly shuddering at what I have done and what will be done to me,—this is the list of the benefits of which the executioner will deprive me.

Ah, no matter! It is horrible!

IV.

The black carriage transported me here, into this hideous Bicêtre. [24]

[24] Formerly a prison, now an insane asylum for old men.

Seen from a distance, this edifice has a certain majesty. It unrolls itself in the horizon in front of a hill, and from afar retains something of its former splendor, an air of a king's castle.

But as you approach it, the palace becomes a paltry ruin. The cut-away gables offend the eye. An impoverished and ignominious aspect sullies these royal façades; the walls seem to be afflicted with leprosy. No panes of glass in the window frames, but massive bars of iron crossing and recrossing each other, upon which are pressed here and there the haggard face of a wretch condemned to the galleys or of a madman.

It is life, seen when close upon it.

V.

I had hardly arrived when iron hands seized upon me. Precautions of every sort were multiplied. Neither knife nor fork for my meals. The strait-jacket—a species of sail-cloth bag—imprisoned my arms. They answered for my life. I had appealed against my sentence. This tiresome affair might last six or seven weeks longer. It was important to keep me safe and sound for the Place de la Grève.

The first days they treated me with a gentleness which was horrible to me. The kindness of the jailor smelt of the scaffold. Fortunately, at the end of a few days, habit took the upper hand; they confounded me with the other prisoners in a common brutality, and had no more for me those unaccustomed politenesses which brought the executioner continually before my eyes. This was not the only change for the better. My youth, my docility, and, above all, a few Latin words which I addressed to the gate-keeper, who did not understand them, granted to me the weekly promenade of the other prisoners, and caused the strait-jacket which paralyzed me to disappear. After long hesitation, they at last consented to give me ink, paper, and pens, and a night-lamp.

Every Sunday, after church service, they let me loose in the yard, at the hour of recreation. There I talk with the other prisoners; I cannot avoid it. They are kindly enough, these wretches. They relate to me their adventures. They give one the horrors, but I know they boast. They teach me to talk *argot*, to *rouscailler bigorne*, as they call it. It is a complete language grafted upon the general language like a hideous excrescence—a monstrous wart. Sometimes there is a singular and frightfully picturesque energy in this language. "*There are crushed grapes on the path*" means, "*Blood in the road*." To marry the widow is to be hanged, as if the gibbet's rope were the widow of all the hanged men. The head of a thief has two names—*la sorbonne*, when it meditates; *la tronche*, when it is cut off by the guillotine. Sometimes there is the spirit of the vaudeville in these expressions:—The *willow cachemire* (the rag-woman's basket), *the liar* (the tongue), and then, continually strange, mysterious, sordid, ugly words, dug up from no one knows where:—*the taule* (the executioner), *the cóne* (death), *the closet* (the place of execution). They seem the toads and spiders of the fairy tale falling from their lips. When you hear this language spoken, it produces the effect of dirty and dusty fragments—of a heap of ragged clothing shaken out before you. At least, these men pity me, and they alone. The jailers, the cell-keepers,—I wish them no harm,—talk and laugh before me as if I were a thing.

VI.

I said to myself,—

Since I have the means of writing, why should I not write? But write what? Shut in between four walls of cold, bare stone, without liberty for my footsteps, without horizon for my eyes, for sole diversion mechanically occupied in following, all day long, the slow march of the whitish square which the wicket of my door defined opposite to it on the sombre wall, and, as I said a little while ago, alone with a single idea—an idea of crime and of punishment, of murder and of death! Can I have anything to say—I, who have no more anything to do in this world? And what can I find in this empty and shattered brain which is worthwhile recording?

Why not? If everything around me is monotonous and discolored, is there not within me a tempest—a struggle—a tragedy? This fixed idea which possesses me, does it not present itself to me every hour, every moment, under a new form, always more hideous and more bloody, as the time draws near? "Why should not I attempt to say to myself all that I experience of the violent and the unknown in the abandoned situation in which I am placed? Certainly, the material is rich; and, abridged though my life may be, there still remains in the terrors, in the tortures, which will fill up its measure, enough to wear out this pen—to dry up this inkstand. Besides, in this anguish, the only means to suffer less from it is to observe it. To paint it will prevent me from feeling it.

And then, what I shall thus write will not, perhaps, be useless. This journal of my sufferings, hour after hour, minute after minute, torture after torture,—if I have the strength to carry it out up to the moment when it will be physically impossible to continue it,—this history, necessarily unfinished, but as complete as possible, of my sensations, will it not bear with it a great and profound teaching? Would there not be, in this indisputable record of the dying thought, in this always-increasing progression of griefs—in this sort of intellectual autopsy of a condemned criminal—more than one lesson for those who condemn? Perhaps the perusal of it may cause them to act less lightly, when, at some other time, they may be called upon to decide whether a head which thinks—the head of a man—shall be cast into what they call the scales of justice. Perhaps these men have never reflected upon slow succession of tortures which is comprised in the rapid formula of the death sentence. Have they ever even been arrested by this painful idea, that in the man they thus cut off there exists an intelligence—an intelligence which counted on living—a soul which is not prepared for death? No! They only see in all this the vertical fall of a triangular knife, and think, without doubt, that for the criminal there is nothing before, nothing after. These pages will undeceive them. Published some day, perhaps, they may direct their attention for a few moments to the sufferings of the mind; for those are precisely what they do not seem even to suspect. They are triumphant in being able to kill without causing the body to suffer. As if this were the great question to be resolved! What is physical pain in comparison with moral suffering! Horror and pity, laws thus made! A day will perhaps come, and perhaps these memoirs—last confidences of a wretch—may contribute. . . Provided that, after my death, the wind may not play in the prison-court with these bits of paper, soiled with mud, or that they may not come to rot in the rain, pasted in stars on the broken window-pane of a jailer.

VII.

That what I write here may one day prove useful to others, that it may arrest the judge ready to give judgment, that it may save unhappy creatures, innocent or guilty, from the agony to which I am condemned—why? What good will it do me? What matters it? When my head shall have been cut off, what is it to me that others are cut off afterwards? Is it possible that I can have had such foolish fancies? To overturn the scaffold after I have mounted it! I ask you what profit will it bring to me?

What! the sun, the spring-time, the fields full of flowers, birds with their morning songs, light clouds, trees, nature, liberty, life,—all these no longer are mine. Ah, it is I who ought to be saved! Is it really true that it can be so, that I must die tomorrow, today, perhaps? O God! what a horrible idea! to break one's skull against the wall of a dungeon!

VIII.

Let me see what is left to me. Three days of delay after the judgment has been pronounced, to allow me to appeal.

Eight days of forgetfulness before the bar of the criminal court, after which, the papers, as they are called, are sent to the minister. Fifteen days of waiting in the minister's office, the minister not even being aware that these papers exist, but who is nevertheless supposed to transmit them after examination to the court of appeals.

Then classification, numbering, registering, for the guillotine is encumbered, and no one must pass out of his turn.

Fifteen days of observation that you may not have been served out of your turn.

At last the court meets, usually upon a Thursday, rejects twenty appeals in a lump, and returns them all to the minister, who sends them again to the prosecuting attorney, who sends them to the executioner. Three days.

The morning of the fourth day, the attorney's substitute says, while adjusting his cravat, "This affair must be brought to a close." Then if the clerk's substitute has no engagement to breakfast with friends which hinders him, the order for the execution is minuted, revised, a fair copy written off, and is sent to its destination,—and the next day at dawn a noise of hammering may be heard on the Place de la Grève, and in the public places hoarse criers announcing the news.

Six weeks in all. The young girl was right.

But it is at least five weeks, perhaps six, that I have been in this cell at Bicêtre, and it does not seem to me more than three days. It was Thursday.

IX.

I have just made my will. What for? I am condemned to pay the expenses, and all that I have will hardly suffice. The guillotine costs dear.

I leave a mother, I leave a wife, I leave a child.

A little girl of three years, gentle, rosy, delicate, with large, black eyes, and long chestnut-colored hair.

She was two years and one month old when I saw her for the last time.

Thus, after my death, three women without a son, without a husband, without a father,—three orphans different in kind,—three widows made by the law.

I admit that I am justly punished. These innocent creatures, what have they done? No matter, they are dishonored; they are ruined. This is justice.

My poor mother does not give me great anxiety. She is sixty-four years old; the blow will kill her. Or, if she holds on a few days longer, she will say nothing, provided they give her the means of keeping warm to the last.

Neither do I feel great uneasiness about my wife. She is already in feeble health, and is not strong-minded. She will die, too.

Unless she goes mad. They say that keeps one alive; but, at least, the intelligence feels nothing. It is asleep; it is as if dead.

But my daughter, my child, my poor little Mary, who laughs, and plays, and sings, at this moment, and thinks of nothing,—this is what cuts me to the heart!

X.

Here is a description of my dungeon. Eight feet square, four walls of hewn stone resting at right angles on a stone pavement raised one step above the outer passage.

To the right of the door on entering is a sort of recess which is a mockery of an alcove. A bundle of straw is thrown into it, and upon this the prisoner is supposed to rest and to sleep, clad in linen trousers and waistcoat, in winter and in summer.

Over my head, instead of the sky, a black vault in *ogive*—that is what it is called—from which are suspended thick spider-webs, hanging down like rags.

For what remains, no windows, not even an airhole; a door, the wood of which is hidden by iron.

I forget,—in the centre of the door, towards the top, an opening of nine square inches with a grating in form of a cross, and which the turnkey can shut up at night.

Outside, a tolerably long passage, lighted and aired by means of narrow loop-holes at the top of the wall, and divided into compartments of masonry which communicate with each other by a series of low-arched doors; each one of these compartments serves as a sort of antechamber to a dungeon similar to mine. It is in these dungeons that prisoners, condemned by the director of the prison to disciplinary punishment, are shut up. The first three cells are reserved for prisoners condemned to death, because, being nearest to the entrance, it is more convenient for the jailer.

These dungeons are all that remain of the ancient chateau of Bicêtre, as it was built in the fifteenth century by Cardinal Winchester, he who had Joan of Arc burned. I heard this said by some curious visitors who came the other day to look at me in my box, and who gazed at me from a distance as they would at a wild beast in a menagerie. They gave the turnkey five francs.

I forgot to say that, night and day, there is a sentinel on duty at my door, and that I cannot raise my eyes to the square opening in the door without finding two eyes fixed and staring at me.

And they take for granted that there is light and air enough in this stone chest.

XI.

Since daylight has not yet appeared, what can I do with the rest of the night? An idea just presents itself. I have got up, and passed my lamp all along the four walls of my cell. They are covered with writings, with drawings, with strange faces, and names which are mixed up and efface each other. It seems that each occupant wished to leave some trace of himself—here, at least. Pencil marks, chalk, charcoal, letters black, white, and grey, sometimes cut deep in the stone, here and there rusty characters, as if written with blood,—certainly, if I had a clearer head, I would take great interest in this strange book which unrolls itself to my eyes, page after page, upon each stone of this dungeon. I would like to recompose a whole with these fragments of thought scattered upon stone, to find each man under each name, to restore sense and life to these mutilated inscriptions, to these dismembered phrases, to these truncated syllables,—heads without bodies, like those who wrote them.

On a level with the head of my bed, there are two hearts pierced by an arrow, and above, "*Love until death.*" The poor fellow did not make a long engagement.

On one side a sort of three-cornered hat, with a little figure coarsely drawn beneath it, and these words, "*Vive L'Empereur*. 1824."

Other burning hearts, with this inscription, characteristic in a prison, "*I love and adore Mathieu Danvin*, Jacques."

Upon the opposite wall may be read this word, "*Papavoine*." The capital P is embroidered with arabesques and embellished with care.

A couplet of an obscene song. A liberty-cap, cut pretty deeply into the stone, with this underneath, "*Bories,—La Republique*." He was one of the four sergeants of La Rochelle. Poor young man! How hideous are their pretended political necessities! For an idea, for a dream, for an abstraction, this horrible reality called the guillotine! And I who complain, I—wretch—who have committed a veritable crime, who have shed blood,—I will not continue my research further. I have just seen, pencilled in white in a corner of the wall, a frightful picture,—the figure of that scaffold which, at this hour, perhaps, is being set up for me. The lamp almost fell from my hands.

XII.

I turned again and seated myself precipitately on my straw, my head bowed down between my knees. Then my childish fright passed away, and a strange curiosity induced me to continue my readings on the wall.

By the side of the name of Papavoine I tore away an enormous spider-web, thickened with dust, and stretched across the angle of the wall. Under this web there were four or five names, perfectly legible, among others of which nothing remains but a stain on the wall: "*Dautun*, 1815." "*Poulain*, 1818." "*Jean Martin*, 1821." "*Castaing*, 1823." I read these names, and lugubrious memories came back to me. Dautun is he who cut up his brother into quarters and went at night about Paris, throwing the head into a fountain, the body into a sewer. Poulain assassinated his wife. Jean Martin shot his father at the moment that the old man opened his window. Castaing, the doctor, who poisoned his friend, and who, treating him for the disease he had caused, repeated the dose instead of giving the remedy. And, after these, Papavoine, the horrible madman who killed children by cutting their heads open with a knife.

These, said I, while a shiver of fever spread through my veins, these are they who were the occupants of this cell before me. Here, upon the same pavement where I am seated, they have thought their last thoughts, these men of murder and of blood! Along this wall, in this narrow square, their last steps have trod like those of a wild beast. They succeeded each other, at short intervals. It appears that this dungeon is never vacant. They have left their place yet warm, and it is I to whom they have left it. I will go in my turn to rejoin them in the cemetery at Clamart, where the grass grows so rank.

I am neither visionary nor superstitious. It is probable that these ideas brought on fever; but while I was in this reverie, it seemed to me all of a sudden that these fatal names were written in fire on the black wall, a ringing more and more rapid burst out in my ears,—a reddish light filled my eyes, and then it seemed to me that the dungeon was full of men—of strange men—who carried their heads in their left hands and held them by the mouth because they had no hair. All shook their fists at me, except the parricide.

I closed my eyes with horror, but I only saw all more distinctly.

Dream, vision, or reality, I should have gone mad if a sudden impression had not awakened me in time. I was just about to fall over backward, when I felt crawling on my foot a cold body and velvety paws. It was the spider I had disturbed, which was making its escape.

This dispossessed me. Oh, the frightful spectres! No, it was a vapor, an imagination of empty and convulsive brain,—chimeras such as came to Macbeth. The dead are dead,—that is certain. They are firmly padlocked in the sepulchre,—a prison that cannot be broken. How could I have been so afraid? The gate of the tomb does not open inwardly.

XIII.

I have seen within the past few days a hideous thing. It was hardly light, and the prison was full of noise. Opening and shutting of heavy doors, creaking of bolts and iron padlocks, jingling of keys hanging at the waists of the turnkeys, trembling of the stairs under the hasty steps, and voices calling and answering from one end to the other of the long corridors. My dungeoned neighbors, those who were on punishment, were gayer than usual. All Bicêtre seemed to laugh, sing, run, and dance.

I alone mute amidst this uproar, alone motionless in this tumult; astonished and attentive I listened.

A jailer passed.

I ventured to call to him, and ask if it was holiday in the prison.

"Holiday if you choose to call it so," he replied. "It is today that the galley-slaves, who are to leave for Toulon tomorrow, are to be ironed. Would you like to see it? It will amuse you."

In truth, for a solitary recluse, any sort of spectacle, however odious, is a piece of good fortune. I accepted the amusement.

The turnkey took the usual precautions to make sure of me, then conducted me into a little empty cell, absolutely without furniture, which had a grated window—a veritable window—of the usual height above the pavement, and through which the sky could really be seen.

"Here we are," said he; "from here you will see and you will hear. You will be all alone in your box, like the king."

Then he went out, and closed upon me locks, padlocks, and bolts.

The window looked upon a square and tolerably extensive court, around which rose on the four sides a great building of hewn stone, six stories high. Nothing can be imagined more degraded, more naked, more miserable to the eye than this quadruple façade, pierced with a multitude of grated windows to which were pressed eagerly from top to bottom, a crowd of wasted, pale visages, crowded one against the other, like the stones in a wall, and all, so to say, framed in the crossings of the iron bars. They were the prisoners, spectators of the ceremony while awaiting their turn to be actors. They might have been taken for souls in misery at the gates of purgatory, which look out upon hell.

All looked in silence upon the still empty court. They were waiting. Among these sullen and deadened faces, here and there shone out a pair of keen, piercing eyes, like points of fire.

The square of prisons which surrounds the court does not close up entirely. One of the four fronts of the edifice (that which looks to the east), is cut apart near the middle, and is joined to its other half by an iron gate. This gate opens into a second court, smaller than the first, which is also blocked in with walls and blackened gables.

All round the principal court stone benches are built against the walls. In the middle is a stem of curved iron, intended to support a lantern.

Twelve o'clock struck. A large carriage door, hidden under a deep recess, opened suddenly. A cart, escorted by a sort of dirty, shabby soldiery, in a blue uniform with red epaulettes and yellow shoulder-belts, entered the court heavily, with a noise of rattling iron. It was the overseer of the band and the chains.

At the same instant, as if this noise awakened all the noises of the prison, the spectators at the windows, until then silent and motionless, broke out into cries of joy, songs, menaces, and imprecations, mingled with bursts of laughter horrible to listen to. It was easy to believe that all these faces were those of demons on a masquerade. Upon each visage there appeared a grimace, every fist was thrust out of the grating, every voice howled, every eye shot out flame, and I was terrified to see so many sparks reappear in these ashes.

Meanwhile the sergeants—among whom might be distinguished by their clean dress and by their agitation, a few curious persons from Paris, who desired to be present incognito—went tranquilly to work. One of them mounted on the cart, and threw to his comrades the chains, the travelling collars, the packages of linen trousers. They then distributed the work. Some went to stretch out, in one corner of the court, the long chains, which, in their slang, they called the strings; others spread upon the pavement the taffetas, that is, the shirts and trousers; whilst the most sagacious examined, one by one, under the eye of their captain, a short, thick-set, old man, the irons for the wrists and ankles, which they proved by making them resound against the pavement. All this, to the railing acclamations of the prisoners, whose voices were only overcome by the roaring laughter of those for whom these preparations were being made, and who were seen at the windows of the old prison which was upon the little court.

When these preliminaries were terminated, a gentleman in a dress embroidered with silver, whom they called Mr. Inspector, gave an order to the director of the prison, and a moment after, two or three low doors vomited out at the same time, and as if by gusts, into the court, swarms of hideous, yelling, ragged men. These were the condemned to the galleys.

On their entrance, double cries of joy at the windows. Some among them, the great names of the galleys, were saluted with acclamations and applause, which they received with a sort of modest pride. Most of them wore a kind of hat which they had woven for themselves out of the straw of their dungeon—always of some strange form, so that in the cities through which they might pass the hat might attract attention to the head under it. Those were still more applauded. One, above all the others, excited transports of enthusiasm,—a young man seventeen years old, who had the face of a young girl. He came out of his dungeon, where he had been in solitary confinement for a week; but of his bundle of straw he had made himself a garment which covered him from his head to his feet, and he came into the court wheeling about with the agility of a serpent. He was a mountebank, who had been condemned for stealing. There was a mad clapping of hands and screaming with pleasure at his appearance. The other galley-slaves responded; it was a horrible thing, this exchange of gaieties between the actual galley-slaves and those who aspired to that honor,—although society itself was present, represented by the jailors and terrified assistants, present from curiosity. Crime laughed in its face, and of this horrible chastisement made a family gala day.

As they arrived, they were pushed between two hedges of guards into the smaller court, where the examination of the surgeon awaited them. This, because all made a last effort to escape the journey, alleging some excuse of ill health, weak eyes, a lame leg, a mutilated hand. But they were almost always found fit for the galleys, and then each one resigned himself with indifference, forgetting in a few minutes his pretended infirmity from birth.

The gate of the little court reopened. A keeper called the roll in alphabetical order, and then they marched out, one by one, each man going forward and taking his place, standing in a corner of the great court, next a companion given to him by the chance of his initial letter. Thus each man is reduced to himself; each one bears his chain for himself, side by side with an unknown being; and if by chance a galley-slave should have a friend, the chain separates them. Last of sufferings!

When about thirty men had taken their places, the gate was shut. A sergeant put them in line with his stick, threw down before each of them a shirt, a waistcoat, and trousers, of coarse linen; then made a sign, and all commenced to undress themselves.

An unexpected incident, as if by express order, came to change this humiliation to torture.

Until now the weather had been rather fine, and if the October wind cooled the air from time to time, it opened in the grey mists of the skies a crevice from whence shot forth a ray of sunshine. But hardly had the men stripped themselves of their rags, and at the moment that they presented themselves naked and upright to the suspicious inspection of the keepers and to the curious looks of the strangers who walked round them to examine their shoulders, the sky blackened, a cold autumnal shower burst forth suddenly and discharged itself in torrents into the square court, on the uncovered heads and naked bodies of the felons, and upon their wretched garments spread out on the ground before them.

In a twinkling the yard was cleared of all who were neither sergeant nor galley-slave. The sightseers from Paris took shelter under the projecting doorways.

Meanwhile, the rain fell in torrents. Nothing could be seen but the naked and dripping men standing on the drowned pavement. A sullen silence had succeeded to their blustering bravados. They shivered, their teeth chattered, their thin legs, their knotty knees, shook under them; and it was pitiful to see them apply themselves to covering their blue members with the soaked shirts, waistcoats, and trousers, dripping with rain. Nakedness would have been better.

One only, an old man, kept up his courage. He cried out, while wiping himself with his wet shirt, that "*this was not on the programme.*" Then he broke out into a laugh, and shook his fist at the sky.

When they had put on their travelling-clothes, they were led in bands of twenty or thirty to the other corner of the yard, where cords stretched out on the ground were ready for them. These cords are long and strong chains cut transversely every two feet by other short chains, at the extremity of which is a square iron instrument which opens at one angle by means of a hinge, and is shut at an opposite angle by an iron ball riveted on the neck, during the whole journey. When these chains are spread out on the ground, they represent very fairly the large backbone of a fish.

The galley-slaves were made to sit down in the mud, on the drenched pavements; their collars were tried on; then two smiths of the service, supplied with, portable anvils, riveted them cold, with heavy blows of an iron club. This is a frightful moment, in which the boldest turn pale. Each blow of the hammer falling upon the anvil supported by the back, makes the chin of the patient rebound. The slightest movement backward would crush in his skull like a nut-shell.

After this operation they became gloomy. Nothing more was heard but the clattering of the chains, and, at intervals, a cry, and the dull sound of the stick of the overseer upon the limbs of the refractory. Some of them wept; the old men shuddered and bit their lips. I looked with terror upon all these sinister profiles, in their iron frames.

Thus, after the inspection of the doctor, that of the jailer, then the irons. Three acts to this drama.

A ray of sunshine reappeared. It might be said to have set all these brains on fire. All of the men rose at once, as if by a convulsive movement. The five gangs took hold of hands, and, in a moment, formed an immense ring around the pole of the lantern. They turned around until it fatigued the eyes to look at them. They sang a song of the galleys—a slang ballad—to an air now plaintive, now furious and gay. At intervals shrill cries, screams of broken, panting laughter, mixed themselves with mysterious words; then furiously mad applause; and the chains clanking together in cadence, served as an orchestra to songs hoarser even than its noise. If I sought an image of a witches' revel, I would wish it neither better nor worse.

A large tub was now brought into the yard. The overseer broke up the dance by blows from his stick, and conducted the men to this tub, in which were to be seen bits of herbs floating in a sort of smoking and dirty liquid. They eat.

Then, having eaten, they threw upon the ground what remained of their soup and of their black bread, and went again to singing and dancing. It seems that tins liberty is allowed them the day of the riveting the irons and the following night.

I was observing this strange spectacle with a curiosity so eager, so palpitating, so attentive, that I entirely forgot my own position. A profound sentiment of pity moved me to the heart's core, and their laughter made me weep.

Suddenly, in the midst of the profound reverie into which I had fallen, I saw the howling crowd stop and become silent. Then every eye turned to the window which I occupied. "He's condemned to death! condemned to death!" they screamed, pointing at me with their fingers; and the explosions of joy were again redoubled.

I stood petrified. I do not know from whom they knew me, or how they had recognized me.

"Good morning! good evening!" they cried out to me with an atrocious sneer. One of the youngest, condemned to the galleys for life, with a shining, leaden face, looked at me with envy, saying, "He is lucky; he will be *clipped!* Adieu, comrade!"

I cannot tell what terrible thing passed within me. I was, in fact, their comrade. La Grove is a sister of Toulon. I was even in a lower position than they. They did me honor. I shuddered.

Yes, their comrade! and, a few days later, I, too, should be a spectacle for them!

I had remained at the window, motionless, deprived of the use of my limbs, paralyzed; but when I saw the five chain-gangs approach me with words of an infernal cordiality—when I heard the tumultuous rush of their chains, of their clamors, of their steps at the foot of the wall, it seemed to me that this swarm of demons was forcing my wretched cell. I uttered a cry. I threw myself against the door with a violence which nearly broke it open; but there were no means of escaping. The bolts were drawn outside. I beat upon it. I screamed with rage. Then I seemed to hear, nearer and nearer still, the frightful voices of the men. I thought I saw their hideous heads already on the edge of my window-sill. I uttered a second cry of anguish, and fell back in a swoon.

XIV.

When I came to myself it was night. I was lying on a cot. A lantern which glimmered from the ceiling gave enough light for me to see other cots in a line with my own. I understood that they had brought me into the infirmary. I remained a few moments awake; but without thought and without memory, absorbed by the happiness of being in a bed. It is quite sure that in other days this prison-hospital bed would have made me shrink with disgust and pity; but I was no longer the same man. The sheets were brown and rough to the touch, the covering thin and ragged; I could feel the hard straw bed through the upper mattress. What did that matter? My limbs could stretch out at ease under these coarse sheets, under this covering, thin though it was. Little by little I felt the horrible cold to the marrow of my bones to which I was accustomed, begin to dissipate. I again fell asleep.

I was awakened by a loud noise. The day was beginning to break. This noise came from without. My bed was beside a window. I sat up to see what it was.

The window looked upon the great court of Bicêtre. This court was full of people; two lines of veteran troops had great difficulty in keeping a narrow road, which crossed the court, free in the midst of the crowd. Between this double line of soldiers, moved slowly, jolted by every stone, five long carts filled with men. They were the galley slaves who were setting out on their journey.

These carts were uncovered. Each gang occupied one. The men were seated back to back along the edge of each side of the carts, separated by the common chain, which was stretched lengthwise in the cart. A sergeant, armed with a loaded gun, stood with his foot resting upon the extremity of this chain. The scraping of the irons was heard, and, at each jolt of the vehicle, their heads and their pendent legs were seen to shake from side to side.

A fine, penetrating rain, froze the air; and their linen trousers, already turned from gray to black, stuck to their knees. Their long beards, their close-cut hair, ran with water. Their faces were purple! I could see them tremble with the cold, and gnash their teeth with rage. More than this, no possible movement. Once riveted to this chain, a man is only a fraction of this hideous whole called the gang, which moves like a single man.

Intelligence must abdicate; the irons of the galleys condemn it to death; and, as to the animal left, he must have neither appetites nor necessities, except at fixed hours. Thus motionless, the most of them half naked, heads uncovered and feet hanging down, they commence their journey of twenty-five days, heaped together in the same cart, clothed with the same garments under the leaden sun of July or under the freezing rains of November. It might be said that man calls upon the heavens to do half of his work of vengeance.

There arose between the crowd and the carts a horrible kind of dialogue, which I could not hear,—abuse on one side, bravados on the other, curses from both; but, at a sign from the captain, I saw a shower of blows descend hap-hazard into the carts, upon shoulders and heads, and all was reduced to that sort of external calm which is called *order*; but eyes were full of vengeance, and the fists of the wretches were doubled up upon their knees.

The five carts, escorted by military on horseback and overseers on foot, disappeared successively under the arched door of Bicêtre; a sixth cart followed, in which shook about pell-mell, kettles, copper cooking-utensils, and reserve chains. Several over Beers, belated at their breakfast, ran out to rejoin their squad. The crowd melted away. All this spectacle vanished like a phantasmagoria. By degrees the sounds weakened, the heavy noise of wheels and the horses' feet on the paved road to Fontainebleau, the cracking of the whips, the rattling of the chains, and the yells of the people who were wishing ill luck to the travellers, soon died away in the distance.

And this is but the commencement for them!

What could my lawyer have been thinking of? The galleys! Rather death a thousand times! The scaffold rather than the galleys! Annihilation rather than hell! Far better to give up my neck to Guillotin's knife than to the iron collar of the chain-gang. The galleys! Just heaven!

XV.

Unhappily, I was not sick. The next day I was obliged to leave the infirmary. The dungeon again took possession of me.

Not sick—no! I am young, healthy, and strong,—my blood flows freely in my veins, all my limbs obey the least of my caprices, I am robust in body and spirit—constituted for a long life; and yet I have an illness, a mortal illness—an illness made by the hand of man!

Since I left the infirmary a heart-rending idea has come to me,—an idea which nearly drives me mad: it is that I might have made my escape if they had let me remain there. Those doctors, those sisters of charity appeared to take an interest in me. To die so young and by such a death! One might think that they really pitied me they came so kindly to my bedside. Bah!—curiosity! And then those people who cure can cure easily of a fever, but not of a death sentence; and then it would have been so easy for them—a door opened! What would it have been to them?

No more chances now! My appeal will be rejected because all is in order. The witnesses have testified well, the advocates have pleaded well, the judges have judged well. I do not count on it unless—no folly, no more hope! An appeal is a cord which keeps you suspended over an abyss, and which you hear cracking every instant until it breaks. It is as if the knife of the guillotine took six minutes to fall.

If I had my pardon! My pardon! and through whom? and why? and how? It is impossible that they pardon me. The "example," as they say.

I have only three steps to take—Bicêtre, the Conciergerie, the grave!

XVI.

During the few hours I passed in the infirmary I sat near a window in the sun—it had come forth again—or at least receiving from the sun all that the bars of the window let in to me.

I was there, my head heavy and burning, between my two hands, which had more than they could bear, my elbows on my knees, my feet on the bars of my chair, for my depression is so great that I am bowed down, and I double myself up as if I had neither bones in my limbs nor muscles in my flesh.

The smothering air of the prison suffocated me more than ever. I still had in my ears all this noise of the chains. I experienced a great fatigue of Bicêtre. It seemed to me that God ought to take pity on me and send me at least a little bird to sing to me opposite on the ledge of the roof.

I do not know whether it was God or the demon who granted my prayer; but at the same moment I heard under my window a fresh voice—not that of a bird, but still better—the fresh, pure, velvety voice of a young girl of fifteen. I raised my head with a start. I listened eagerly to the song which she was singing. It was a slow, mournful air, a sort of sad, lamenting strain. Here are the words,—

"It was in Mail Street
Where they nabbed me,
    Malury!
Three pals of the king,
    Lirlonfa, Maluretta,
They put on the bracelets,
    Lirlonfa, Malury!"

I cannot express the bitterness of my disappointment. The voice continued,—

"They put on the bracelets,
    Malury!
They caught and held me fast,
    Lirlonfa, Maluretta,
They broke down my castle,
    Lirlonfa, Malury!
And as I went along,
    Lirlonfa, Maluretta,
I met a bosom friend,
    Lirlonfa, Malury!

A bosom friend in need,
    Malury!
'Begone and tell my half,
    Lirlonfa, Maluretta,
That they have grabbed me,
    Lirlonfa, Malury!

My half in fury came,
    Lirlonfa, Maluretta,
She said, 'What now, my man?'
    Lirlonfa, Malury!

She said, 'What now, my man?'
    Malury!
I have sweated an oak tree,
    Lirlonfa, Maluretta,
I have done up in a case,
    Lirlonfa, Malury,
His trunk and his bark,
    Lirlonfa, Maluretta,
And the three have me fast,
    Lirlonfa, Malury!

And all there was of him,
    Malury!
My half hot to Versailles,
    Lirlonfa, Maluretta,
And at feet of majesty,
    Lirlonfa, Malury,
Wrung her hands and cried,
    Lirlonfa, Maluretta,
To get me back again,
    Lirlonfa, Malury!

To get me back again,
    Malury!
Ah, if ever I get loose,
    Lirlonfa, Maluretta,

My half in silk and satin,
    Lirlonfa, Malury,
And gay head-gear,
    Lirlonfa, Maluretta,
And red shoes shall go,
    Lirlonfa, Malury!

And red shoes shall go,
    Malury!
But, great chief in a rage flies,
    Lirlonfa, Maluretta,
Says, 'By the crown I wear,
    Lirlonfa, Malury,
'I'll make him dance a jig,
    Lirlonfa, Maluretta,
Where there is no floor for his feet,
    Lirlonfa, Malury!'"

I did not listen, and could have listened no further. The half-hidden, half-understood of this horrible Complaint, [25] this struggle of the brigand with the constables, this thief which he meets and whom he despatches to his wife, this horrible message, "I have assassinated a man and I am arrested, *I have sweated an oak tree, and the three have me fast!*"—this woman who runs off to Versailles for a pardon, this majesty who gets angry and menaces the prisoner to make him dance "*Where there is no floor for his feet*" and all this sung to the sweetest tune and with the sweetest voice that ever soothed human ear! I remained stricken, frozen, annihilated! It was so frightfully repulsive, all those monstrous words falling from those fresh vermilion lips. It was the slime of the snail on a rose.

[25] Every time there is an execution in France a "Complaint" of this sort is hawked about the streets. Sometimes these terrible facetiæ are admirably written, probably by some well-known author, whose name is, of course, never made public, and always with a certain frightful pleasantry.

I cannot express what I felt. I was at the same time wounded and soothed. The slang of the den and of the galleys—this grotesque and bloody language, this hideous compound blended with the voice of a young girl—graceful transition from the voice of the child to that of the woman!—all these ill-made, deformed words, sung—cadenced—dropped like pearls!

Ah, a prison has something infamous about it! There is a venom which soils everything in it. Everything withers under its influence,—even the song of a girl of fifteen! You find a bird there,—there are stains upon its wings. You gather a flower, you would breathe its freshness,—it stinks.

XVII.

Oh, if I could escape, how I would run across the fields! Now, I must not run. I should be looked at and suspected. On the contrary, I must walk slowly, my head high, and singing. Must try to get an old smock-frock, blue and red. All the gardeners in the neighborhood wear such. It would disguise well.

I know, near Arcueil, a clump of trees, close by a marsh, where, when I was at college, I went with my companions on Thursdays to fish for frogs. I would hide myself there until evening.

At nightfall I would set out again. I would go to Vincennes,—no, the river would prevent me,—I would go to Arpajon. It would have been better to take the road to St. Germain and proceed to Havre, where I could embark for England. No matter! I reach Longjumeau; a policeman passes; he asks me for my passport. I am lost! Ah, unhappy dreamer, break first through the three feet of stone wall which imprison you! Death! death!

When I think that I came here to Bicêtre when I was a little child to see the great well and the mad people!

XVIII.

While I was writing all this my lamp has grown, pale, daylight is come, the chapel clock has struck six.

What does this mean? The turnkey on guard has just entered my dungeon. He took off his cap, bowed to me, excused himself for interrupting me, and asked me, softening as much as possible his rough voice, what I would like for breakfast.

I was seized with a chill. Can it be for today?

XIX.

It is for today!

The director of the prison himself has been to make me a visit. He asked me in what way he could be useful or agreeable to me; expressed a desire that I might have no complaint to make of subordinates; inquired with interest after my health, and how I had passed the night. On his leaving me he called me "Mr.!"

It is for today!

XX.

This jailer does not believe that I have any complaint to make, either of him or his under-jailers. He is right; it would be wrong in me to complain. They have followed their trade; they have kept me safe; and then they have been polite at my coming and at my going. Ought I not to be satisfied?

This good jailer, with his benignant smile, with his soft words, his eye which flatters and spies, his large, heavy hands, is the prison incarnate. Bicêtre transformed into a man. All is prison around me! I find the prison under every form; under the human form as under that of the grating and the bolt. This wall is the prison in stone; this door is the prison in wood; these turnkeys are the prison in flesh and blood. The prison is a species of being, horrible, complete, indivisible,—half house, half man. I am its prey; it gloats over me; it enlaces me in all its folds; it encloses me in its granite walls, locks me up with its iron locks, and watches over me with the eyes of the jailer.

Ah, wretch that I am, what is to become of me? What do they intend to do with me?

XXI.

I am calm now. All is finished,—entirely finished! I am relieved from the horrible anxiety into which the director's visit threw me; for, I confess, I hoped still. Now, God be thanked! I hope no longer.

This is what took place.

At the moment that half-past six struck—no, it was the quarter—the door of my cell reopened. A white-headed old man, in a brown coat, entered. He opened his coat; I saw a cassock and band. It was a priest. This priest was not the chaplain of the prison. That was an ill omen.

He sat down opposite to me, with a benevolent smile, then shook his head, and raised his eyes to heaven,—that is to say, to the vault of the dungeon. I understood him.

"My son," said he, "are you prepared?"

I replied, in a feeble voice,—

"I am not prepared, but I am ready."

Nevertheless my sight grew dim; a cold sweat broke out all over me; I felt my temples swell, and I had my tars full of heavy ringings.

While I wavered back and forth on my chair, like one asleep, the good old man spoke, or at least it seemed so to me, and I have a sort of recollection that I saw his lips move, his hands gesticulate, and his eyes brighten.

The door opened a second time. The noise of the bolts tore us away, me from my stupor, him from his discourse. A sort of gentleman in a black coat, accompanied by the director of the prison, presented himself, and saluted me profoundly. This man had upon his visage something of the official sadness of the hired pall-bearers at a funeral. He held a roll of paper in his hand.

"Sir," said he, with a courteous smile, "I am a sheriff of the royal court of Paris. I have the honor of bringing you a message from the prosecuting attorney."

The first shock was over. All my presence of mind came back to me.

"It is Mr. Prosecutor who asked so promptly for my head," replied I; "he does me much honor in writing to me. I hope that my death will give him great pleasure; for it would be hard for me to believe that a thing he solicited with so much ardor can be entirely indifferent to him."

I said all this, and then resumed, with a firm voice,—

"Read, sir!"

He set to reading a long manuscript, singing at the end of each line and hesitating in the middle of every word. It was the rejection of my appeal.

"The sentence will be executed today, on the Place de la Grève," added he, on terminating, without raising his eyes from his stamped paper. "We set out at half-past seven, precisely, for the Conciergerie. My dear sir, will you have the goodness to follow me?"

For several moments I had ceased listening. The director was talking with the priest. My interlocutor had his eyes fixed upon his paper. I looked at the door, which had remained half open. Ah, wretch that I am! four soldiers, with their guns, in the corridor!

The sheriff had repeated his question, looking at me this time.

"As you please," I replied to him; "I am at your disposal."

He bowed to me, saying,—

"I will have the honor of coming for you in half an hour."

Then they left me alone.

Some way of escape, my God,—any way! I must get away—I must immediately—by the doors, the windows, the supports of the roof—even if I should leave my flesh on the rafters!

Oh, furies! demons! maledictions! It would take months to pierce these walls with good tools, and I have not a nail,—not an hour!

XXII.

In the Conciergerie.

Here I am *transferred*, as the legal document has it.

But the journey is worth relating.

Half-past seven o'clock struck when the messenger again presented himself on the sill of my dungeon.

"Sir," said he, "I am waiting for you."

Alas, he and others!

I rose, and made one step forward. It seemed to me that I could not make a second, my head was so heavy and my legs so weak. However, I recovered myself, and continued with a pretty firm gait. Before quitting my cell I gave a last look to its walls. I loved my dungeon. And then, I left it vacant and open, which gives a strange aspect to a dungeon.

As for that, it will not remain so long. Someone is expected this evening, say the turnkeys,—a criminal whom the court is doing for at this present moment.

At a turn in the corridor the chaplain joined us. He had just breakfasted.

On leaving the jail, the director took my hand affectionately, and reinforced my guard with four veterans.

Before the door of the infirmary a dying old man called out to me, "We will meet again!"

We reached the court-yard. I breathed. The air did me good.

We did not walk long. A carriage drawn by four post-horses was stationed in the first court. It was the same that had brought me here, a sort of oblong cabriolet, divided into two sections by a transverse grating of iron wire, so thick that it seemed to have been knit. The two sections have each a door, one at the back, the other in the front of the cabriolet. All so dirty, so black, so dusty, that the hearse for the poor is a coronation-coach in comparison to it.

Before burying myself in this tomb on two wheels, I cast a glance into the court,—one of those glances of despair before which it seems that the very walls ought to crumble.

The court-yard, a little space planted with trees, was even more encumbered with spectators than for the galley-slaves. Already the crowd!

As on the day of the departure of the chain-gang, a fine, cold rain fell, such, as is now falling,—which will fall, probably, all day,—which will last longer than I will.

The paths were ploughed up, the court was full of mud and water. It pleased me to see the crowd in that marsh.

We got in, the sheriff and the guard in the front compartment,—the priest, myself, and a guard in the other. Four guards on horseback around the vehicle. Thus, without counting the postillion, eight men for one man.

While I was getting into the carriage, there was an old woman with grey eyes, who said, "I like that better than the chain-gang."

I can imagine that. It is a spectacle that can be taken in more easily at a glance. It is quicker seen. It is quite as fine a sight, and more convenient. Nothing takes off the attention. There is only one man, and in this single man as much misery as in all the galley-slaves at once. Only it is less dispersed. It is a concentrated liquor, much higher flavored.

The vehicle jolts. It has made a dull noise in passing under the vault of the great entrance. Then it has turned into the avenue, and the heavy double gates of Bicêtre have closed behind it. I felt myself driven off in a sort of stupor, like a man fallen into a trance, who can neither move nor cry out, but who feels that they are burying him.

I heard vaguely the little bells hung round the neck of the post-horses ring in cadence, or by spasms; the iron wheels grind against the pavement, or strike the body of the carriage, in avoiding the ruts in the road; the sonorous gallop of the guard about the cabriolet; the cracking whip of the postillion. All this seemed to be a whirlwind, which was bearing me away. Through the grating of the little window opposite to me my eyes were fixed mechanically upon the inscription engraved in large letters over the great gate of Bicêtre, "*Hospice de la Vieillesse.*"

"Indeed," said I to myself, "there are people who grow old there!"

And, like a person between waking and sleeping, I turned this idea over and over in my spirit, deadened by grief. Suddenly, the vehicle, in passing from the avenue to the high road, changed the point of view of the window. The towers of Notre Dame came blue and half visible through the mist of Paris into the narrow frame. Immediately the point of view of my spirit changed also. I became a machine, like the vehicle. To the idea of Bicêtre succeeded that of the towers of Notre Dame. "Those who are where the flag floats from the tower will see me plainly," said I to myself, smiling stupidly.

I think it was at this moment that the priest began to talk again. Patiently I let him go on. I had already in my ears the sound of the wheels, of the gallop of the horses, of the whip of the postillion. It is only one noise more.

I listened in silence to this outpouring of monotonous words, which soothed my thoughts like the murmur of a fountain, and which passed before me always changing and always the same, like the twisted elms on the high road, when the sharp, dry voice of the sheriff seated in the front, came suddenly to arouse me.

"Well, Mr. Abbé"," said he, in a tone of voice almost gay, "what have you heard new?"

He turned to the priest, as he spoke.

The chaplain, who went on talking without interruption, and who was deafened by the noise of the vehicle, did not reply.

"Eh! eh!" returned the sheriff, raising his voice to get the advantage over the wheels, "infernal carriage!"

Infernal, in truth!

He continued,—

"Doubtless it is the jolting,—there is no hearing. What was I saying? Will you be so kind as to tell me what I was saying, Mr. Abbé? Ah, do you know the important news of Paris, today?"

I shuddered, as if he were speaking of myself.

"No," replied the priest, who had at last heard. "I have not had time to read the papers this morning. I will see what it is this evening. When I am occupied in this way all day, I tell my porter to keep my papers, and I read them when I go in."

"Bah!" replied the sheriff. "It is impossible that you have not heard it. The news of the day,—the news of this morning."

I took up the conversation.

"I think I know it."

The sheriff looked at me.

"You, indeed! In that case what do you say to it?"

"You have a great deal of curiosity," I replied.

"Why, sir," returned the sheriff, "everyone has his own political opinion. I esteem you too highly not to believe that you have one also. As for my part, I am entirely in favor of the re-establishment of the national guard. I was sergeant of my company, and it was very pleasant—"

I interrupted him.

"I did not think that was the matter in question."

"And what then? You said you knew the news."

"I was speaking of another affair which occupies Paris this morning."

The fool did not understand. His curiosity was awakened.

"Another piece of news? Where the devil could you hear news? What is it, I beg, sir? Do you know what it is, Mr. Abbé? Are you better informed than myself? Let me know it, I pray. What is it about? You see I like the latest news. I relate all I hear to the president of the court, and it amuses him."

And a torrent of idle stuff. He turned alternately to the priest and myself, and I only replied by shrugging my shoulders.

"Well, well," said he. "Of what are you thinking?"

"I think," replied I, "that this evening I shall think no more."

"Ah, that is it," he retorted. "You are too sad. Mr. Castaing was talkative."

Then, after a pause,—

"I accompanied Mr. Papavoine. He kept on his cap, and smoked his cigar. As to the young fellows of La Rochelle, they only talked to each other; but they talked."

He made another pause, and pursued,—

"Madmen! Enthusiasts! They looked as if they despised all around them. As for you, young man, I find you very thoughtful."

"Young man!" returned I. "I am older than you! Each quarter of an hour which slips away makes me a year older."

He turned and looked at me some moments, with a foolish amazement. Then set to sneering, audibly.

"Go away! You are laughing at me! Older than I! I might be your grandfather!"

"I have no desire to laugh," replied I, gravely.

He opened his snuff-box.

"Come, come, dear sir, do not get angry with me. Take a pinch of snuff, and do not let me have your ill-will."

"Do not be afraid. It would not last long."

At this moment his snuff-box, which he handed me, struck the grating which separated us. A jolt caused it to strike against it violently. It fell, with its contents, at the feet of the guard.

"Curse the grating!" exclaimed the sheriff.

He turned to me. "Am I not unlucky! Here is all my snuff lost."

"I lose more than you," replied I, smiling.

He tried to gather up his snuff, grumbling between his teeth,—

"More than I do! That is easily said. No snuff until I get to Paris. It is terrible!"

The chaplain then addressed him a few words of consolation; and I do not know whether I was preoccupied, but it seemed to me that they were the continuation of the exhortation of which I had had the commencement. By degrees the conversation was established between the priest and the sheriff. I let them talk, while I continued to think.

On approaching the gates of the city, I was, doubtless, still abstracted, but Paris seemed to be making more noise than usual.

The vehicle stopped a moment in front of the city custom-office. The city inspectors examined it. If it had been a sheep, a beef which they were carrying to the slaughter-house, a purse of money would have been required, but a human head does not pay entrance-tax. We passed on.

After crossing the boulevard, the cabriolet drove on briskly into the old winding streets of the Faubourg St. Marceau and of the Cité, which twist and interlace each other like the thousand paths of an ant-hill. Upon the pavement of these narrow ways the rolling of the vehicle grew so noisy and so rapid that I heard nothing else of the movements outside. When I cast my eyes without, through the little square loop-hole, it seemed to me that passers stopped to look at the vehicle, and that children ran after it. I seemed also, from time to time, to see an old man or woman standing in the squares with their hands full of packages of printed sheets which the passers-by eagerly claimed, while the vendors opened their mouths to cry out.

Half-past eight struck the great clock of the Palace at the moment that we reached the Court of the Conciergerie. The sight of this great stairway, these sinister doorways, froze my blood. When the vehicle stopped I thought that the beating of my heart would stop also.

I gathered up my strength. The door opened, with the rapidity of lightning. I jumped out of the rolling dungeon, and I disappeared with great strides under the arched way between two hedges of soldiers. A crowd had already collected on my passage.

XXIII.

Whilst I marched on in the public galleries of the Palace of Justice, I felt almost free and at my ease; but all my fortitude abandoned me when opened before me the low doors, the secret stairways, the interior passages, the long, dull, smothery corridors, into which only those who condemn or who are condemned ever enter.

The sheriff still remained with me. The priest left me, to be back again in two hours. He had his affairs to attend to.

I was led to the cabinet of the director, in whose hands the sheriff placed me. It was an exchange. The director requested him to wait a moment, announcing that he had some *game* to hand over to be sent to Bicêtre, on the return of the gig. Doubtless the criminal condemned today,—the one who is to sleep tonight on the bundle of straw I had not had time to wear away.

"Good," replied the sheriff to the director. "I will wait awhile. We can make out the two reports at once. That is very convenient."

While waiting they put me in a little closet, opening into the director's room. There I was left alone, well bolted in.

I do not know what I thought about, nor how long I had been there, when a rough, violent burst of laughter, sounding in my ears, awoke me from my reverie.

I raised my eyes, shivering. I was no longer alone in the cell.

A man was with me. A man about fifty-five years old, of middle height, wrinkled, bent, and gray,—with thickset limbs, a squint in his gray eyes, a bitter laugh on his face,—dirty, ragged, half naked, repulsive to behold.

It seems that the door had opened, had vomited him, and then shut again, without my perceiving it. If death could come to me in this way!

We looked at each other fixedly for some seconds, the man and myself, he prolonging his laugh, which sounded like a death-rattle,—I, half astonished, half frightened.

"Who are you?" said I to him, at last.

"A droll question," he replied. "A *friauche*."

"A *friauche!* What does that mean?"

This question renewed his merriment.

"That means," cried he, in the midst of a burst of laughter, "that the *taule* will play in the basket with my *sorbonne* in six weeks, just as it will with your *tronche* in six hours. Ha! ha! it appears that you understand now."

In fact I was pale, and my hair stood on end. He was the other condemned criminal,—the one of today,—the one who was expected at Bicêtre—my heir.

He continued, "How can I help it? Here is my history. I am the son of a good thief! It is a pity that Charlot [26] took it upon himself to tie his cravat for him one morning. It was in the times when the gallows reigned, by the grace of God. At six years old I had neither father nor mother. In summer I made wheels in the dust on the roadside, so that travellers might throw me a cent from the windows of their carriages. In winter I went barefooted in the mud, blowing my red fingers. My skin was visible through my poor rags. At nine years I commenced to use my *louches* (hands). Now and then I emptied a *fouillousse* (a pocket). I stole a cloak. At ten years I was a thief. Then I made acquaintances. At seventeen I was a housebreaker. I robbed a shop. I made false keys. I was caught. I was old enough, so I was sent *to row in the little navy*,—the galleys. It is a hard life; to sleep on a board, to drink nothing but water, to eat black bread, to drag a ball which is of no use. Strokes from a stick and strokes from the sun. Besides all that, they shave your head. I who had such handsome chestnut hair! Never mind; I served my time, fifteen years; they drag on all the same. I was thirty-two years old. One fine morning they gave me my passport and sixty-six francs which I had saved up during my fifteen years of the galleys by working sixteen hours a day, thirty days a month, and twelve months in the year. No matter, I wanted to be an honest man with my sixty-six francs, and I had more fine sentiments under my ragged clothes than are always to be found under the priest's cassock. But the devil take their passport! It was yellow, and they had written upon it *liberated galley-slave*. I was forced to show this everywhere, and to present it once a week to the mayor of the village that I was forced to inhabit. Fine recommendation,—a galley's man! I frightened everyone. Little children ran away from me. Everybody shut their doors at my approach. No one would give me work. I eat up my sixty-six francs, and then I was obliged to live on. I showed my arms, how strong they were for work. Every door was closed. I offered my day's labor for fifteen cents, for ten cents, for five cents,—no one would take me. What to do? One day I was hungry; I broke the windows of a baker; I seized a loaf of bread, and the baker seized me. I did not eat the bread, and I was sent to the galleys for life, with three letters of fire on my shoulder. I will show them to you, if you like. They call that justice, *recidive!* And now I am a *returned horse*. They sent me again to Toulon,—this time with a green cap. I was obliged to escape. To do that I had only three walls to cut through, and two chains to cut. I had one nail. I escaped. They fired the alarm-gun, for we fellows are like the cardinals at Rome,—we are dressed in red and they fire guns when we depart. They burnt their powder to no purpose. This time no yellow passport, but no money either. I met with comrades who had also served their time, or broken their *thread*. Their chief asked me to join them. They assassinated on the high roads. I accepted, and set to work to kill in order to live. Sometimes it was a diligence, sometimes a post-chaise, sometimes a cattle-dealer on horseback. We took the money and let the beast or the carriage go loose, and we buried the man under a tree, taking care that the feet were well covered, and then we danced on the grave so that the earth might not appear freshly turned up. I grew old in that way, hiding in the bushes, sleeping under the starlight, tracked from wood to wood, but at least free and belonging to myself alone. Everything must have an ending, and as well this as any other. The string merchants (the mounted police) one fine night took us by the collar. My comrades ran away, but I, the oldest of them, I remained in the claws of these cats with gold-laced cocked hats on. They brought me here. I had already mounted all the rounds of the ladder, one excepted. To steal a handkerchief or to kill a man was all the same to me.

There was one more *recidive* for me. I have only to pass through the hands of the *reaper*. My business was soon done. In fact, I began to grow old and good for nothing. My father married the widow (was hung). I retire to the Abbey of Mount Regret (the grave). This is all, comrade."

[26] The executioner.

    I remained stupid, while listening to him. He commenced to laugh louder still than when he came in, and wanted to take my hand. I drew back with horror.
    "Friend," said he, "you do not look brave. Don't go to playing the poltroon. You see it is a bad moment, but it is quick over. I wish I might be there first, to show you the somersault. Thousand gods! I am almost inclined not to appeal if they will cut me off today with you. The same priest will serve for both of us. It is nothing to me to take your leavings. You see what a good fellow I am, eh! Say, will you accept my friendship!"
    He made another step towards me.
    "Sir," said I, repelling him, "I thank you."
    Renewed bursts of laughter at my response.
    "Ha! ha! Sir, you are a marquis! He is a marquis!"
    I interrupted him.
    "My friend, I have need to collect my thoughts. Leave me quiet."
    The gravity of my speech made him thoughtful at once. He shook his almost bald gray head. Then, digging with his nails at his hairy breast, through his open shirt,—
    "I understand," he murmured, between his teeth. "The wild boar" (the priest).
    Then, after a few moments' silence,—
    "Look here," said he, almost timidly, "you are marquis, which is all well enough, but you have on a very handsome coat which will be of very little use to you. The man will take it. Give it to me. I will sell it, to get some tobacco."
    I took off my coat and gave it to him. He clapped his hands, with the delight of a child. Then, seeing that I was in my shirt, and that I shivered,—
    "You are cold, sir. Put on this. It is raining, and you will be wet; and then one must look decent in the cart."
    While thus speaking, he took off his heavy woollen vest, and passed my arms into it. I let him do as he wished.
    Then I leaned against the wall, and I cannot describe the effect this man had on me. He set to examining the coat that I had given him, and every moment uttered cries of joy. "The pockets are quite new,—the collar is not at all worn. I will get at least fifteen francs for it. What luck! Tobacco for my whole six weeks."
    The door reopened. They had come for us both,—me to conduct to the room in which condemned criminals await the hour; him to bear off to Bicêtre. He took his place, laughing, in the midst of the guards, and saying,—
    "Take care! Don't make a mistake! We have exchanged peelings,—this gentleman and myself. Do not take me in his place. The devil! That would not suit me at all, now that I have something to buy tobacco with."

XXIV.

This old scoundrel! He took my coat, for I did not give it to him, and has left me this rag, his disgusting vest. Who will I look like?

I did not let him take my coat, either through indifference or through charity. No,—simply because he was stronger than I. If I had refused him, he would have beaten me with his great fists.

Charity, forsooth! I was full of the most wicked sentiments! I could have strangled him with my hands, the old robber! I could grind him under my feet!

I feel my heart full of rage and bitterness. I believe my gall-bag is broken. Death makes man wicked.

XXV.

They have led me into a cell in which there are only the four walls, with no end to bars at the window and bolts at the door, as may be supposed.

I asked for a table, a chair, and writing materials. They brought all these to me.

Then I asked for a bed. The turnkey gave me a look, which signified, "What for?"

However, they set up a cot bed in a corner. But at the same tune a guard came and took his place in what they call *my room*. Are they afraid that I will strangle myself with the mattress?

XXVI.

It is ten o'clock!

Oh, my poor little daughter! In six hours I shall be dead! I shall be something unclean, which will be dragged about on the dissecting-table. On one side a head that they will mould. On the other a trunk that they will dissect. Then with what is left, they will fill up a coffin, and all will go to Clamart!

This is what they will do with your father, these men, none of whom hate me, all of whom pity me, and would save me if they could. They are going to kill me. Do you comprehend that, Mary? To kill me in cold blood, with ceremony, for the good of the thing! Ah, great God!

Poor little one! Your father who loved you so much; your father who kissed your sweet, white neck; who continually ran his hands through your silken curls; who took your pretty little face in his hands; who made you trot on his knees; and who in the evening joined your little hands in prayer to God!

Who will do all this for you now? Who will love you as he does? All the children of your age will have fathers, except yourself. How can you grow unaccustomed, my child, to the new-year's gifts, the pretty playthings, the sugar-plums, the kisses? How will you forget, unhappy orphan, that you must eat and drink?

Oh, if these jurors had seen you, my pretty little Mary, they would have understood that they must not kill the father of a child of three years.

And when she will be grown up, if ever she is, what will become of her? Her father will be one of the recollections of the people of Paris. She will blush for me and for my name. She will be despised, repulsed, vile, because of me,—of me, who love her with all the tenderness of my heart! Oh, my little darling Mary! Can it be true that you will be ashamed of me,—will hold me in horror!

Wretch that I am! What a crime I have committed, and what a crime I cause society to commit!

Ah, is it indeed true that I am to die before the close of the day? Is it indeed true that this is I? This dull sound of cries I hear without; this flood of joyous people, who already hurry along the quays; these guards, who are preparing in their barracks; this priest, in his black gown; this other man, with red hands. They are for me! It is I who am to die! I, the same who am here,—who live, who move, who breathe, who am seated at this table, which resembles any other table, and might be elsewhere. I, in truth that I, whom I touch and feel, and whose garments fall in these folds!

XXVII.

If I only knew how it is done, and in what way they lie on it! It is horrible that I do not know it.

The name of the thing is frightful, and I cannot understand it. I have never been able to write or pronounce it.

The combination of these ten letters,—their aspect, their physiognomy,—are made to awaken a perfectly frightful idea, and the physician of hateful memory who invented the thing had a predestined name.

The image which attaches itself to the word is hideous, vague, undetermined, and all the more sinister. Each syllable is like a piece of the machine I construct and demolish incessantly in my own brain this monstrous carpentry.

I do not dare to ask any questions about it, but it is frightful not to know what it is, nor how it acts. It appears that there is a sort of scale, and that they make you lie on the belly. Ah, my hair will turn white before my head falls!

XXVIII.

I saw it once, however.

I was passing the Place de la Grève in a carriage, one day, about eleven o'clock in the morning. All of a sudden the carriage stopped.

There was a crowd upon the Place. I put my head out of the window. The populace crowded the Grève and the quays, and there were men, women, and children, standing on the parapets. Over these heads might be seen a sort of platform in red wood, which three men were engaged in putting up.

A criminal was to be executed during the day, and they were building the machine.

I turned my head aside before having fully seen. At the side of my carriage there was a woman, who was saying to a child,—

"Look! look! The knife does not slip well. They are going to grease the groove with a candle-end."

It is probable that is what they are doing now. Eleven o'clock has just struck. Doubtless, they are greasing the groove.

Ah, this time, unhappy man, you will not turn your head away!

XXIX.

Oh, my pardon! my pardon! Perhaps they pardon me! The king has no ill-will against me. Send someone at once for my lawyer! Quick,—my lawyer! I will accept the galleys. Five years of the galleys, let that be enough,—or twenty years,—or for life, with the hot iron, but leave me my life!

A galleys-man walks,—he goes and comes,—he sees the sun.

XXX.

The priest has come back.

He has white hair, a mild look, a good, respectable face; he is, in fact, an excellent and charitable man. This morning I saw him empty his purse into the prisoners' hands. Why is it that his voice has nothing in it that touches or that seems touched? How is it that he has said nothing yet which reached either my intelligence or my heart?

This morning I was wandering. I hardly heard what he said. Nevertheless, his words seemed useless, and I was indifferent. They ran off like that cold, cold rain, on that glass window-pane.

However, when he came back, just now, the sight of him did me good. "Among all these men, he is the only one who remains a man to me," said I to myself. And I am seized with an ardent thirst for good, consoling words.

We took our seats,—he upon the chair, I upon the bed. He said to me,—

"My son,—"

This word opened my heart. He continued,—

"My son, do you believe in God?"

"Yes, my father," replied I to him.

"Do you believe in the Holy Catholic, Apostolic and Roman Church?"

"Willingly," said I.

"My son," said he, "you appear to doubt."

Whereupon, he began to speak. He spoke a long time. He said a great number of words. Then, when he thought he had finished, he rose and looked at me, for the first time since the beginning of his discourse, interrogating me,—

"Do you think this?"

I protest that I listened first with avidity, then with attention, and at last with devotion.

I rose also.

"Sir," I said, "leave me alone, I beg of you."

He asked me,—

"When shall I come back?"

"I will let you know."

Then he went out without speaking, but shaking his head, as if he said to himself, "A scoffer."

No, low as I am fallen, I am not a scoffer; and God is witness that I believe in him.

But what did this old man say to me? Nothing feeling,—nothing which could move,—nothing which wept,—nothing torn from the soul,—nothing which came from his heart and went to mine,—nothing from him to me. On the contrary, a something vague, unmarked, applicable to everything,—emphatic where it ought to have been profound,—flat where it should have been simple,—a species of sentimental sermon,—a theological elegy,—here and there a Latin quotation,—St. Augustin, St. Gregory, and the rest of them. And then he seemed to be saying a lesson recited twenty times before, going over a theme obliterated in his memory from being too well known. Not a look in the eye, not a tone in the voice, not a gesture of the hands.

And how could it be otherwise? This priest is the official chaplain of the prison. His trade is to console and to exhort. He lives by it. The culprits, the felons, are the springs of his eloquence. He confesses them and assists them, because he has his round to accomplish. He has grown old while leading men to death. He has long become habituated to what others shudder at. His well powdered hair no longer stands up with terror. The galleys and the scaffold are every-day things to him. His sympathies are worn out. Probably he has his register; on such a page, the felons; on such others, the condemned to death. He receives notice one day that the next, at a given hour, there will be someone to console. He asks which it may be, one condemned to the galleys or to death. He reads over the page, and then he comes. In this fashion it comes to pass that those who go to Toulon and those who go to the Grève are mere commonplaces for him, and he is a mere commonplace thing to them.

Let them, instead of that, go and search out some young vicar, some old priest in the nearest parish, take him from his fireside where he may be reading, expecting nothing, and let them say to him,—

"A man is about to die, and you are needed to console him. You must be with him when they tie his hands, when they cut off his hair. You must get into the cart with him, and hide the executioner with your crucifix. You must be jolted with him by the stones of the pavement until you reach the Place de la Grève. You must pass through the horrible, bloodthirsty crowd, with him. You must embrace him at the foot of the scaffold, and you must stay with him until his head is cast on one side, his body on the other."

Then let them bring this priest to me, palpitating, shivering from head to foot. Let them cast me into his arms, at his feet. He will weep, and we will weep together; and he will be eloquent, and I will be consoled. My heart will be melted into his. He will take possession of my soul, and I will accept his God.

But this good old man, what is he to me? What am I to him? An individual of an unhappy species,—a shadow, like so many others that he has seen,—a unit to add to the number of executions.

I am, perhaps, wrong to repulse him thus. He is good, and I am wicked. Alas, it is not my fault! It is the breath of my condemned nostrils which spoils and destroys everything.

They have just brought me some nourishment. They thought I needed it. A delicate and choice repast,—a fowl, I believe, with other things. I have tried to eat; but at the first mouthful everything fell from my lips, it seemed Bo bitter and disgusting.

XXXI.

A gentleman has just been in here, who kept his hat on his head, and who hardly noticed me. He opened a measuring-rule and set about measuring from bottom to top the stones in the wall, saying from time to time, in a loud voice, "That is it," or, "No, that will not do."

I asked the guard who he was. It appears that he is a sort of sub-architect employed in the prison.

On his side, his curiosity was awakened with regard to me. He exchanged a few broken sentences with the turnkey, who accompanied him; then, fixing his eyes for a moment upon me, and shaking his head in an indifferent manner, he turned again to taking his measures, and to his loud expressions.

This task finished, he approached me and said, with his piercing voice,—

"My good friend, in six months this prison will be in a much better condition."

And his gesture seemed to add, "You will not be here to enjoy it,—what a pity!"

He almost smiled. I began to think he was about to jest with me pleasantly, as they rally with a bride on her wedding-day.

My guard, a veteran soldier, took upon himself to reply.

"Sir," said he, "it is not decent to speak so loud in a dying man's room."

The architect took leave. I remained, like one of the stones he was measuring.

XXXII.

After this, a ridiculous incident happened. They changed guard, and my good sentinel, with whom I did not even shake hands, selfish that I am, was replaced by another with a low forehead, expressionless eyes, and almost idiotic face.

I paid no attention to him, however. My back was turned to the door, as I was seated at the table. I tried to cool my brow with my hands. My thoughts bewildered me.

A slight touch upon the shoulder caused me to turn my head. It was the new sentinel, with whom I remained alone.

This is as near as possible the manner in which he addressed me,—

"Criminal, have you a kind heart?"

"No," said I.

The roughness of my response appeared to disconcert him. However, he recommenced, hesitatingly,—

"No one is wicked for the pleasure of the thing."

"Why not?" I replied. "If that is all that you have to say to me, let me alone. What are you aiming at?"

"I beg your pardon, my criminal," returned he. "I want only two words with you. This is it. If you could make a poor man happy, would you refuse to do it?"

I shrugged my shoulders.

"Are you just out of Bedlam? You make choice of a singular vessel to draw your happiness out of. I make anyone happy!"

He lowered his voice and put on a mysterious look, entirely out of harmony with his foolish face.

"Yes, criminal, yes! Happiness, yes,—fortune, everything,—will come from you. You see I am nothing but a poor police guard. The service is heavy, the pay is light. So I put into a lottery to counterbalance. I must have some sort of a trade. Until now, all that I have wanted to make me win is a good number. I hunt every where to find the right ones, and I always fall just one short. I get 76,—the 77 draws. I try again and again,—mine does not come. A little patience, if you please. I am almost done. Now, this is a fine chance for me. It appears, criminal, that you are to be done for today. It is certain that the dead see beforehand the numbers that will be drawn. Promise me to come tomorrow evening,—what will it be to you?—and tell me three numbers, three good ones. Eh! I am not afraid of ghosts, you may be sure. This is my address, 'Barracks Popincourt, Staircase

A, No. 26, at the end of the corridor.' You will recognize me, won't you? Come this evening, if it will suit you better."

I would have disdained to answer this imbecile, if a wild hope had not crossed my brain. In the desperate position in which I found myself, one is tempted to believe that a chain may be severed with a hair.

"Listen," said I, acting a part as well as it is possible for one who looks death in the face. "I can, in fact, make you richer than the king,—make you win millions,—but on one condition."

He opened his stupid eyes.

"What is it? What is it? Anything to please you, my criminal."

"Instead of three numbers, I promise you four. Change clothes with me."

"If that is all," cried he, commencing to loosen the first buttons of his uniform.

I rose from my chair. I observed all his movements. My heart beat aloud. I already saw before me the doors opening at the sight of my guard's uniform, and the Place and the street and the Palace of Justice behind me.

But he turned, with a look of indecision.

"But it is not to go out of here."

I saw that all was lost. Nevertheless, I made a last effort,—useless and impossible.

"Yes, but your fortune is made."

He interrupted me.

"No, indeed! No, indeed! And my numbers! To make sure of their being good, you must be dead."

I reseated myself, mute, and more despairing from the hope I had had.

XXXIII.

I have closed my eyes, I hold my hands upon them, and try to forget the present in the past. Whilst I dream, the recollections of my childhood and my youth come back to me, sweet, calm, and smiling, like islands of flowers floating over this gulf of black and confused thoughts which whirl in my brain.

I see myself a child, a schoolboy, laughing and ruddy, playing, running, crying out with my brothers in the green alley of the wild garden in which my first years were passed,—the enclosure of an ancient convent above which towers with leaden crown the sombre dome of the Val de Grace.

And then, four years later, I am still there, yet a child, but dreamy and full of passion. There is a young girl in the solitary garden.

The little Spanish maiden, with her large eyes and her long hair, her golden-brown skin, her red lips, and her rosy cheeks,—the Andalusian of fourteen years—Pepa.

Our mothers told us to go and run in the alleys. We have come to walk.

They told us to play, and we prefer to talk. Children of the same age, but not of the same sex.

And yet only a year before, we ran, we wrestled together. I quarrelled with Pepita for the best apple on the tree. I struck her for a bird's nest. She cried, and I said, "It serves you right," and we ran together to complain to our mothers, who blamed us aloud, while approving in their hearts.

Now, she leans on my arm, and I am proud and troubled. "We walked slowly; we spoke low. She let her handkerchief fall. I pick it up for her. Our hands tremble as they meet. She talks of her little birds, of the star which we see in the sky, of the vermilion sunset behind the trees, of her school-friends, of her dress and her ribbons. "We say the most innocent things, and we both blush. The little girl has become a young lady. That evening was a summer evening. We were under the chestnut-trees at the bottom of the garden. After one of those long intervals of silence which filled our promenades, she suddenly left my arm, and exclaimed,—

"Let us take a run!"

I see her yet. She was all in black, in mourning for her grandmother. A childish idea had seized her. Pepa was Pepita again. She said,—

"Let us have a run."

And she ran before me, with her waist delicate as a wasp's, and her little feet, which threw up her dress above her ankles. I ran after her. She flew on. The air, as she ran, blew up her black cape, and allowed me to see her fresh brown neck.

I was quite out of my senses. I caught her, near the old well in ruins. I took her by the waist, in right of victory, and made her sit down on the mossy bank. She did not resist. She was out of breath, and laughing. I was serious, and looked deep into her black eyes, through her long lashes.

"Sit down there," she said. "It is still light enough,—let us read something. Have you a book with you?"

I had in my pocket the second volume of Spallanzani's Travels. I opened at hazard. I drew near her, she leaned her shoulder against mine, and we read together, in a low voice, the same page. Before turning over the page, she was always obliged to wait for me. My thought went more slowly than hers.

"Have you finished?" she would say, when I had hardly begun.

Meanwhile, our heads touched, our hair mingled, our breaths gradually drew nearer, and then suddenly our lips.

When we thought of continuing our reading, the sky was full of stars.

"Oh, mamma, mamma!" said she, on going in, "if you only knew how we ran!"

I kept silent.

"You say nothing," said my mother. "You look sad."

I was in Paradise.

It was an evening that I will remember all my life. All my life!

XXXIV.

An hour has just struck. I do not know which. I do not hear the hammer of the clock very well. I feel as if there was an organ playing in my head. It is my last thoughts that are sounding.

At this supreme moment in which I absorb myself in recollections, I look upon my crime with horror, but I would like to repent still more. I had greater remorse before my condemnation; since, I appear to have place only for thoughts of death. And yet, I would like to repent much more.

While I have dreamed for a moment of all that has passed in my life, and when I come back to the hatchet blow which must terminate it presently, I shudder as if it were new, each time. My happy childhood! My promising youth! Golden staff, the end of which is steeped in blood. Between then and the present there is a river of blood, the blood of the other man and of my own. If, some day, my history is read, after so many years of innocence and happiness, it will be hard to believe in this execrable year, which opens by a crime and closes by its punishment. The story will seem out of joint.

And yet, wretched laws and wretched men! I was not a wicked man! Oh, to die in a few hours, and to think that one year ago, on this day, I was free and pure, and that I took autumnal walks,—that I wandered under the trees, crashing the leaves under my feet!

XXXV.

At this minute, even, there are near me, in the houses which surround the Palace and the Grève, and everywhere in Paris, men who are going and coming, laughing, reading the newspaper, thinking of their business,—merchants who are selling, young girls preparing their dresses for the ball this evening, mothers playing with their children.

XXXVI.

I remember one day, when I was a child, that I went to see the great bell of Notre Dame.

I was already giddy from having mounted the sombre spiral stairs, from having crossed the frail gallery which unites the two towers, from having Paris under my feet, when I entered the cage of stone and woodwork in which hangs the great bell, with its clapper, which weighs a thousand pounds.

I advanced tremblingly over the ill-joined planks, looking from a distance at this clock, so famous among the children and the people of Paris, and remarking with terror that the slate coverings of the projecting roofs which surround the belfry with their inclined planes, were on a level with my feet. At intervals I had a bird's-eye view of the Place of Notre Dame, and people walking about it like ants.

Suddenly the great clock tolled. A profound vibration stirred the air, and made the heavy tower oscillate. The planks danced on the rafters. The noise almost threw me backwards. I staggered, ready to fall and slide down on the eloping slate roofs. In terror I lay down on the planks, holding them tight in my two arms, speechless, breathless, with this formidable tolling in my ears; and, under my eyes, the deep Place upon which crossed and re-crossed the peaceable and enviable foot passengers.

And it seems to me that I am still in the tower of the great bell. I feel at the same time deafened and blinded. Something like the noise of a bell shakes the cavities of my brain, and around me I no longer perceive the even, tranquil life which I have left, and where other men still walk, except at a distance, through the crevices of an abyss.

XXXVII.

The Hotel de Ville is a sinister edifice. With its sharp roof, its strange belfry, its great, white clock-dial, its columned stories, its thousand windows, its stairways worn out by footsteps, its two arches, to the right and to the left, it is there on a level with the Grève,—sombre, melancholy, its face eaten away by age, and so black that it is black in the sunlight.

On execution-days, it vomits forth soldiers from all its doors, and looks at the criminal from all its windows.

And, in the evening, its dial, which marks the hour, remains luminous upon its shadowy façade.

XXXVIII.

It is a quarter past one o'clock. This is what I feel at present,—a violent pain in the head, a coldness in the back, my brow burning. Each time that I rise, or that I lean over, there seems to be a liquid which floats in my brain, and which makes it beat against the walls of my skull.

I have convulsive shiverings; and, from time to time, the pen drops from my hand as if by a galvanic shock.

My eyes burn as if I were in a smoke.

I have pains in my elbows.

Only two hours and forty-five minutes more, and I shall be cured!

XXXIX.

They say it is nothing, that there is no suffering, that it is an easy end, and that death in this way is much simplified.

Ha! what is that dying which lasts six weeks, and this death-rattle a whole day? What are the tortures of this irreparable day, which vanishes so slowly and so fast? What is that scale of tortures which ends in the scaffold?

And this is what they call no suffering?

Are there not the same convulsions, whether the blood flows away drop by drop, or whether the intelligence is extinguished thought by thought?

And then, is there no suffering? Are they sure of that? Who told them so? Do they ever tell the story of a head rising bloody on the edge of the basket, and crying out to the people, "It did not hurt me?"

Are there any who have died after this manner, who have come back to thank them, and to tell them, "It is well invented. Stop there. The machine is a good one."

No, nothing of the sort! Less than one minute, less than one second, and the thing is done. Have they ever put themselves, even in thought, in the place of him who is there at the moment that the heavy axe which falls cuts into the flesh, severs the nerves, breaks the vertebræ. What! Only a half second! The pain is cheated! Horror!

XL.

It is singular that I think incessantly of the king. No matter what I do, no matter how I pretend to myself to have given it up, I have a voice continually saying in my ear,—

"There is in this same city, at this same hour, and not far from here, in another place, a man who has also guards at all his doors, a man unique like thyself among the people, with this difference, that he is as high as thou art low. His entire life, minute by minute, is but glory, grandeur, pleasures, intoxications. All around him is love, respect, veneration. The haughtiest voices speak low to him, the proudest brows are bent to him. He has only silk and gold before his eyes. At this hour he is holding a council of ministers, in which everyone is of his opinion; or, perhaps, he is thinking of the hunt tomorrow, or of the ball this evening, sure that the festival will come at the fixed hour, and, leaving to others the labor of his pleasures. And this man is of flesh and blood like thyself! And to cause at this very instant the horrible scaffold to crumble, and everything to be given back to thee,—life, liberty, fortune, family,—it is only necessary that this man should, with this pen, write the seven letters of his name at the bottom of a scrap of paper; or, even that his state carriage should cross the track of thy cart! And he is good, and he would, perhaps, ask no better, and nothing of the sort will happen!"

XLI.

Well, then, let us take courage before death; let us take this horrible idea by both hands and look it in the face; let us ask a history of what it is; let us know what it would of us; let us turn it over in every way; let us spell out the enigma, and look in advance into the tomb.

It seems to me that as soon as my eyes shall be closed, I shall see a great brightness and abysses of light in which my spirit shall roll forever. It seems as if the heaven will be luminous in its own essence, that the stars will be dark spots, and that instead of being, as for the living, spangles of gold on black velvet, they will appear to be black points on cloth of gold.

Or, perhaps, wretch that I am, there will be a hideous, deep gulf, the sides of which will be hung with darkness and shadows, into which I will fall incessantly, while I see forms moving in shade.

Or, again, on awakening after the blow, I will find myself on a level, damp surface, grovelling in obscurity, and turning over and over, like a rolling head. It seems that there will be a great wind, which will drive me along, and that I shall strike now and then against other rolling heads. There will be here and there pools and streams of a warm and strange liquid,—all will be black. When my eyes in their rotation shall be turned upward, they will only see a sky of shadow, whose thick masses shall weigh upon them, and in the distance great arches of smoke, blacker than the darkness. They will also see, fluttering through the night, little red sparks which, on getting nearer, will become birds of fire; and it will be thus to all eternity.

It may be that at certain dates the dead of the Grève assemble during the dark nights of winter on the Place, which belongs to them. It will be a pale, bloody crowd, and I will not fail to be there. There will be no moon, and we will all speak low. The Hotel de Ville will be there, with its worm-eaten façade, its sharp-cut roofs, and its dial, that have been without pity for us. There will be on the Place a guillotine of hell, upon which a demon will decapitate an executioner. It will be four o'clock in the morning. In our turn we shall be the crowd to look on.

It is probable that it will be thus. But, if those dead come back, under what form will they come? What will they keep of the incomplete and mutilated bodies? Which will they choose? Is it the head or the body which is spectre?

Alas! what does death do with our soul? What nature does it leave it? What does it take away or give to it? Where does it place it? Does it ever lend it eyes of flesh, to look upon earth and weep?

Ah! a priest! A priest who may know this! I want a priest, and a crucifix to kiss!

My God! always the same!

XLII.

I begged him to let me sleep. I threw myself on my bed.

In fact, I had a rushing of blood in my head, which made me sleep. It is my last sleep of this sort.

I had a dream.

I dreamed that it was night. It seemed to me that I was in my study, with two or three of my friends. I do not know exactly which.

My wife was in bed in the chamber next mine, and was sleeping with her child.

We were talking in a low voice, my friends and I, and what we were saying frightened us.

Suddenly I seemed to hear a noise somewhere in the other part of the house,—a feeble, strange, uncertain noise.

My friends had heard as well as myself. We listened. It was like a lock being opened slowly,—like a bolt being sawed with caution.

There was something in it that chilled us. We were afraid. We thought that it was robbers trying to get into my house at this late hour of the night.

We resolved to go and see. I rose. I took the candle. My friends followed me, one by one.

We crossed the bedroom at the side. My wife was sleeping with her child.

Then we reached the parlor. Nothing there. The portraits were motionless in their gilt frames on the red walls. It seemed to me that the door from the parlor into the dining-room was not in its usual place.

We entered the dining-room. We searched it. I walked first. The door on the staircase was closed, the windows also. When we came near the stove I saw that the linen-closet was open, and that the door of this closet was pulled back over the angle of the wall, so as to hide it.

This surprised me. We thought there was someone behind the door.

I reached my hand to this door to shut it. It resisted. Astonished, I pulled harder. It yielded suddenly, and discovered to us a little old woman, her hands hanging down, her eyes closed, motionless, and standing as if glued into the angle of the wall.

There was something hideous in this apparition, and my hair stood on end.

I asked the old woman,—

"What are you doing there?"

She did not answer.

I asked her,—

"Who are you?"

She did not answer, did not stir, and stood with closed eyes.

My friends said,—

"She is, without doubt, the accomplice of those who came in with bad intentions. They made their escape, on hearing us coming. She could not get away, and hid herself there."

One of us pushed her over. She fell. She fell in one mass, like a block of wood,—like a dead thing.

We touched her with our feet. Then two of us lifted her up, and set her against the wall. She gave no sign of life. We screamed in her ears. She remained mute as if she was deaf.

We began to lose patience. There was anger in our terror. One of us said,—

"Put the candle under her chin."

I put the lighted wick under her chin. Then she opened one eye a little,—an eye vacant, dull, frightful, which did not see.

I took away the flame, saying,—

"At gust will you answer, old sorceress? Who are you?"

The eye shut, as of itself.

"This is a little too much to bear," said the others. "The candle again,—again. She must be made to speak."

I put the light under her chin again. Then she opened her two eyes slowly, looked at us one after the other; then, stooping quickly, blew out the candle with a cold breath. At the same moment "I felt three sharp teeth imprint themselves into my hand, in the darkness.

I woke up, shuddering, and bathed in a cold sweat.

The good chaplain was seated at the foot of my bed, reading his prayers.

"Have I slept long?" I asked him.

"My son," he said, "you have slept an hour. They have brought your child to see you. She is in the next room, waiting for you. I would not let them wake you."

"Oh," I cried, "my daughter! Let them bring me my daughter!"

XLIII.

She is fresh and rosy. She has large eyes. She is lovely!

They have dressed her in a pretty, becoming dress.

I took her. I lifted her in my arms. I seated her on my knees. I kissed her hair.

What, did not her mother come with her? Her mother is ill,—her grandmother also. This is well.

She looked at me with astonishment. Caressed, embraced, devoured with kisses, she made no resistance, only casting now and then an uneasy glance at her nurse, who was crying in a corner.

At last, I was able to speak.

"Mary," said I, "my little Mary!"

I pressed her violently against my breast, swollen with sobs.

She gave a little scream.

"Oh, you hurt me, sir!" she said.

"Sir!" It is almost a year since she saw me,—the poor child. She has forgotten me, face, speech, and tones; and then, who could recognize me with this beard, these clothes, and this pallor. What! already effaced from this memory, the only one in which I would wish to live. What, already no longer *father*! To be condemned never to hear this word again,—this word in the language of children so sweet that it cannot remain in that of men,—*papa*!

And yet, to hear it from this mouth once more, only once, this is all that I have to ask in exchange for the forty years of life they take from me.

"Listen, Mary," said I, taking her two little hands in mine. "Are you sure you do not know me?"

She looked at me with her beautiful eyes, and replied,—

"No, indeed!"

"Look again," I repeated. "What, you do not know who I am?"

"Yes," she said, "a gentleman."

Alas! to love ardently only one being in the world, to love her with all your love, to have her before you, who sees you, and who looks at you, speaks to you, and answers you, and who does not know you! To wish for consolation from her only, and that she alone in all the world does not know that you need it, because you are going to die!

"Mary," I began, again "have you a papa?"

"Yes, sir," said the child.

"Well, and where is he?"

She opened her large eyes, in astonishment.

"Oh, don't you know? He is dead."

Then she cried out. I had almost let her fall.

"Dead!" said I. "Mary, do you know what it is to be dead?"

"Yes, sir," she replied. "He is in the ground, and in heaven."

She went on, of her own accord.

"I pray to the good God for him, night and morning, at mamma's knee."

I kissed her on the forehead.

"Mary, say your prayer for me."

"I can't, sir. Nobody says prayers in the daytime. Come this evening to my house, and I will say it for you."

I could not bear more of this. I interrupted her.

"Mary, I am your papa."

"Ah!" said she.

I added,—

"Would you like me to be your papa?"

The child turned herself away.

"No, my father was a great deal nicer."

I covered her with tears and kisses. She tried to get loose from my arms, crying out,—

"You hurt me with your beard."

Then I put her on my knees again, devouring her with my eyes, and questioned her.

"Mary, can you read?"

"Yes, I can read very well. Mamma shows me how to read my letters."

"Let us see,—read me a little," said I, pointing to a paper which she held crumpled up in one of her little hands.

She threw back her pretty head.

"Oh, but I only know how to read fables."

"Try, all the same. Let us see. Read."

She unfolded the paper, and began to spell, pointing with her fingers.

S-e-n,—sen—T-e-n-c-e,—tence—Sentence.

I tore it from her hands. It was my death sentence which she was reading to me. Her nurse had bought the paper for a cent. It cost me much dearer.

No words can express, what I felt. My violence frightened her. She was almost crying. Suddenly she said to me,—

"Give me back my paper. You see it is to play with."

I gave her back to her nurse.

"Take her away."

And I fell back in my chair,—sombre, deserted, despairing. They ought to come for me now. I care for nothing, any more. The last fibre of my heart is broken. I am ready for whatever they wish to do to me.

XLIV.

The priest is a good man. The jailer, also. I think they shed tears when I told them that my child had been taken away.

It is done. Now I must brace myself, and think firmly of the executioner, of the cart, of the guards, of the crowd on the bridge, of the crowd upon the quay and at the windows, of all that is prepared expressly for me upon that horrible Place de Grève, which might be paved with the heads which it has seen fall.

I believe I have still an hour to habituate myself to all this.

XLV.

All these people will laugh, will clap their hands, will applaud; and among all these men, now free and unknown to the jailers, who run full of joy to an execution,—in all that mass of heads which will cover the place,—there will be more than one predestined to follow mine into the red basket, sooner or later. More than one who comes for me will come again for himself.

For these fated beings, there is a fatal place upon a certain point of the Grève, a centre of attraction, a snare. They move around it until they are at last caught in it.

XLVI.

My little Mary! They have taken her away to play. She looks at the crowd from the window of the carriage, and thinks no longer of that *gentleman*.

I may possibly have time to write a few pages for her, that she may read them some day, and weep, fifteen years later, over today.

Yes, she must know my history from myself. She must know why I leave her a blood-stained name.

XLVII.

MY STORY.

[*Note of the Publisher.*—The leaves of this chapter have never been found. Perhaps, as seems to be indicated by the following pages, the criminal had not time to write them. This idea came to him late.]

XLVIII.

From a room in the Hotel de Ville.

In the Hotel de Ville! So I am here. The execrable journey is over. The Place is there, and beneath the window the horrible populace which barks at me, waits for me and laughs. I hold myself proudly. I brace myself in vain. My heart has failed me.

When I saw, rising high over all the heads, those two red arms, with their black triangle at the end, built up between the two lanterns of the quay, my heart failed me. I asked to make a last confession. They brought me here, and they are gone to fetch the prosecuting attorney. I am waiting for him. It is, at least, that much time gained.

Here is what happened.

Three hours are striking. They have come to tell me that the time has come. I trembled as if I had been thinking of anything else during six hours, during six weeks, during six months. It produced the effect of something entirely unexpected.

They made me cross their passages, and come down their stairways. They pushed me between two grated doors of the ground floor,—a sombre, narrow, vaulted hall, scarcely lighted in rainy, foggy weather. A chair was in the middle. They told me to sit down. I sat down.

There were near the door and against the walls, several persons standing, besides the priest and the guards. And then, three other men.

The first, the tallest and oldest, was stout and had a red face. He wore a frock-coat and a misshapen, three-cornered hat. This was the man.

He was the executioner,—the valet of the guillotine. The two others were his valets.

I was hardly seated when these two came behind, stealthily, like cats. Then, suddenly, I felt cold steel in my hair, and the scissors creaked in my ears.

My hair, cut at random, fell in locks on my shoulders, and the man in the three-cornered hat brushed them off lightly, with his large hand.

Around me, everyone spoke in low tones.

There was a great noise outside, like a shuddering which floated in the air. I thought at first that it was the river, but, by the burst of laughter, I recognized that it was the crowd.

A young man, near the window, who wrote with a pencil upon a portfolio, asked one of the turnkeys what they called what they were doing.

"The criminal's toilette," replied the other.

I understood that tomorrow it would be in the paper.

Of a sudden, one of the valets took off my vest, and the other took my two hands, which hung down at my sides, carried them behind my back, and I felt the folds of a rope wind slowly around my wrists. At the same time, the other untied my cravat. My fine linen shirt, the only fragment of other days which remained to me, made him hesitate an instant. Then he proceeded to cut off the collar.

At this horrible precaution,—at the shock of the steel which touched my neck,—my elbows shivered, and I uttered a half-suppressed groan. The hand of the executioner trembled.

"I beg your pardon, sir," said he. "Did I hurt you?"

These men are very gentle.

The crowd roared still louder, outside.

The stout man, with the mottled face, offered me a handkerchief, steeped in vinegar, to smell.

"Thank you," said I, in as firm a voice as I could command. "It is of no use. I am quite well."

Then one of them stooped and tied my two feet with a fine, slack cord, so as to allow me to make short steps. This cord was attached to the one which tied my hands.

Then the stout man threw my vest around my neck, and tied the sleeves under my chin. All that was to be done there, was finished.

Then the priest approached, with his crucifix.

"Let us go, my son," said he.

The valets took me under the armpits. I rose and walked. My steps were uncertain, and I wavered as if I had two knees to each leg.

At this moment, the external folding-door was opened wide. A furious clamor, the cold air, and the white light rushed in, reaching even me in the shadow. From the sombre grating I saw rapidly, and all at once, through the rain, the thousand howling heads of-the people, heaped pell-mell over the balustrade of the great stone stairway of the Palace. At the right, on a level with the entrance, a line of guards on horseback, the low door only permitting me to see their fore-feet and chests. Opposite me a detachment of soldiers in battle array. At the left, the back of a cart, on which leaned a short ladder.

A hideous picture, fitly framed by a prison door.

I had preserved my courage for this dreaded moment. I made three steps, and I appeared on the sill of the door.

"There he is! There he is!" cried the crowd. "He is coming at last." And those nearest to me clapped their hands. Much as the king is loved, his appearance would create less sensation.

It was a common cart, with a lank horse, and a driver in a blue and red smock-frock, like those worn by the gardeners in the neighborhood of Bicêtre.

The stout man in the three-cornered hat got in first.

"Good-morning, Mr. Samson," called out the children, hanging on the iron railings.

A valet followed him.

"Bravo, Tuesday," the children again cried out.

They both took their place on the front seat. It was now my turn. I mounted with a pretty firm step.

"He keeps a bold face," said a woman, near the guards.

This frightful praise gave me courage. The priest came and took his place by me,— his back turned to the horse. I shuddered at this attention.

They put some humanity in their proceedings.

I wished to look round me,—guards before, guards behind. Then the crowd, the crowd, the crowd,—a sea of heads on the Place.

A detachment of guards on horseback awaited me at the gate of the Palace.

The officer gave the order. The cart and its procession commenced to move, as if urged forward by the yelling of the populace.

We passed the gates. At the moment that the cart turned toward the Pont de Change, the Place burst out into shouts, from the pavements to the roofs, and the bridges and the quays responded with a force sufficient to stir up an earthquake.

It was because the detachment which was waiting, joined the escort.

"Hats off, hats off!" shouted a thousand voices, at once, as if for the king.

Then I laughed horribly, also, and I said to the priest, "Their hats! my head!"

We proceeded in a walk. The flowers in the market on the quay perfumed the air. The women left their bouquets for me.

Opposite, a little before the square tower which forms the corner of the Palace, there are wine shops, in the upper rooms of which were spectators enjoying their good places,—the women particularly. It must be a good day's work for the shopkeepers.

They hired tables, chairs, scaffoldings, and carts. All bent under the weight of spectators. The dealers in human blood cried out, "Who will have a place?"

A rage against these people took possession of me. I wanted to cry out, "Who wants mine?"

Meanwhile, the cart went on. At each step it made I saw that the crowd broke up behind it; and I perceived, with my haggard eyes, that it formed again on other points of my passage.

On reaching the Pont de Change, I accidentally cast my eyes backwards to the right. My view was arrested by a black tower, on the other quay, high above the houses. This tower was isolated, bristling with sculptures, and on its summit I saw two stone monsters, in profile, seated. I do not know why I asked the priest what this tower was.

"St. Jacques de la Boucherie," replied the executioner.

I do not know how it was that, in spite of the mist and the fine, white rain, which lined the air like the net-work of a spider's web, nothing that went on around me escaped my attention. Each one of these details brought a torture with it. Words fail to depict my emotions.

Towards the middle of the Pont du Change, so wide and so encumbered that we could scarce make our way, a fit of violent horror seized me. I was afraid that I should show my weakness. Last vanity! Then I deadened myself, so as to be blind and deaf to all except the priest, whose words I barely heard, interrupted by clamors.

I took the crucifix and kissed it.

"Have mercy on me, O my God!" And I tried to bury myself in this contemplation.

But each jolt of the rough cart shook me. Then, suddenly, I felt an intense cold. The rain had penetrated my clothing, and wet the skin of my head through my short-cropped hair.

"You are trembling with cold, my son?" asked the priest.

"Yes," I replied. Alas, not only with cold!

At the turn of the bridge the women pitied me, because I was so young.

We had reached the fatal quay. I began neither to see nor hear anything around me. All these voices, all these heads at the windows, at the doors, at the shops, on the lamp-posts,—these eager, cruel spectators,—this crowd, in which all know me and I know no one,—this road paved and walled with human visages. I was drunk, stupid, insensible. The weight of so many eyes upon you is an insupportable agony.

I reeled then on the bench, no longer giving my attention either to the priest or the crucifix.

In the tumult which enveloped me, I could no longer distinguish the cries of pity from those of pleasure,—the laughter from the lamentations,—the voices from any other noise. All, mingled together, formed a din in my brain like an echo of brass.

My eyes read mechanically the signs over the shops.

Once a strange curiosity seized me to turn and see towards what we were approaching. It was a last bravado of the intelligence; but my body would not stir,—my neck was paralyzed as if dead in advance.

I perceived only at one side, to my left over the river, the Tower,—which, if seen thus, hides the other tower.

It was the one from which the flag flies. There were a great many persons on the tower. They must see well from there.

And the cart went on, on, and the shops disappeared, and the signs succeeded each other, written, painted, gilded, and the populace laughed, and pattered in the mud, and I let them go on, as those who are asleep allow themselves to dream.

Suddenly the succession of shops which filled my eyes was cut off at the angle of a Place. The voice of the crowd became louder. The cart stopped suddenly, and I nearly fell, with my face to the planks. The priest held me up.

"Courage," murmured he. Then they brought a ladder behind the cart. He gave me his arm. I got at. Then I made one step, and tried to make another, but I could not. Between the two lanterns of the quay I had seen a sinister object.

Oh, it was the reality which stared me in the face.

I stopped, as if reeling under a blow.

"I have a last declaration to make," said I, feebly.

They brought me up here.

I asked them to let me write my last wishes. They untied my hands; but the rope is here all ready, and the rest is below.

XLIX.

A judge, a magistrate, I do not know of what species, has just come. I asked for my pardon, joining my two hands, and dragging myself on my knees. He answered, smiling fatally, "if that was all I had to say."

"My pardon! My pardon!" I repeated. "Or, for pity's sake, five minutes more."

Who knows? It may come. It is horrible, at my age, to die in this manner. Reprieves have often been known to come at the last moment. "And who should be pardoned, if I may not?

The accursed executioner! He approached the judge to say to him that the execution must be over at a certain hour, and that hour draws near; that he is responsible; and that, besides, it is raining, and there is a risk of rust.

"Ah, for pity's sake, one minute more to wait for my reprieve, or I shall resist, I shall bite."

The judge and the executioner are gone. I am alone. Alone with two guards.

Oh, the horrible people, with their hyena yells. Who knows if I will not escape them? If I will not be saved? If my pardon? It is impossible that I am not reprieved!

Ah, the wicked wretches! They are coming up the stairs!

Four o'clock!

THE END